MORE PRAISE FOR

CAKE TIME

"Siel Ju's *Cake Time* is an astonishing debut. Ju's novel-in-stories is unsettling and fierce and full of loneliness, sadness, and humor. Her voice is so alive, and her candor—particularly about men and sex—is keenly astute, intimate, and startling. The prose is precise and poetic, and Los Angeles vibrates on the page. Wry and heartfelt and uniquely defiant, *Cake Time* is like a hard slap I didn't expect or see coming."

—Victoria Patterson, author of *The Little Brother* and *Drift*

"Siel Ju writes with refreshing candor about sexual appetite and the treacherous difficulty of finding love. There is cruelty in the search and tenderness and a lot of honest fumbling around. *Cake Time* is our time—a provocative debut."

—Noy Holland, author of *BIRD*

"Siel Ju's stories are not boring because they are about not-boring things, like swingers' parties and organic fashion company beauty pageants and high school sex and breakups and hook ups. Lots and lots of breakups and hook ups. I worried for Siel Ju reading about all these breakups and hook ups. Then I reminded myself these are fictions Siel Ju is telling us, and Siel Ju is fine. We are all fine, even after all these breakups and hook ups."

—Elizabeth Ellen, author of *Fast Machine* and *Bridget Fonda*

CAKE TIME

a novel-in-stories

Siel Ju

Red Hen Press | *Pasadena, CA*

Book layout by Selena Trager

Library of Congress Cataloging-in-Publication Data
Names: Ju, Siel, author.
Title: Cake time : a novel-in-stories / Siel Ju.
Description: Pasadena, CA : Red Hen Press, [2017]
Identifiers: LCCN 2016048406 (print) | LCCN 2017007767 (ebook)
   | ISBN 9781597090315 (pbk. : alk. paper)
   | ISBN 9781597095716 (Ebook)
Classification: LCC PS3610.U15 C35 2017 (print) | LCC PS3610.
   U15 (ebook) | DDC 813/.6—dc23
LC record available at https://lccn.loc.gov/2016048406

The National Endowment for the Arts, the Los Angeles County
Arts Commission, the Dwight Stuart Youth Fund, the Max Factor
Family Foundation, the Pasadena Tournament of Roses Foundation,
the Pasadena Arts & Culture Commission and the City of Pasadena
Cultural Affairs Division, the City of Los Angeles Department of
Cultural Affairs, the Audrey & Sydney Irmas Charitable Foundation,
Sony Pictures Entertainment, Amazon Literary Partnership, and the
Sherwood Foundation partially support Red Hen Press.

First Edition
Published by Red Hen Press
www.redhen.org

Acknowledgments

A big thank you to my agent Peter Steinberg. Your support, encouragement, and advice have been and continues to be invaluable to me. Thank you to all my friends and teachers who read these stories in various stages of development: Shilpa Agarwal, Tom Chiarella, Chris Corning, Joe Heithaus, Tanya Knox, Travis Koplow, Edan Lepucki, Paul Mandelbaum, Kathleen Motoike, Carolyn Peters, and Jason Rohrer. And thank you also to Lauren Eggert-Crowe, Zoë Ruiz, and David Rocklin for inviting me to share these stories at your reading series.

For publishing excerpts of the manuscript, thank you to *Eclectica Magazine*, *ZYZZYVA*, *Juked*, and the editors of the anthology *Nothing to Declare: A Guide to the Flash Sequence*.

And finally, thank you to everyone at Red Hen Press!

Contents

CAKE TIME

How Not to Have an Abortion

If suspicious, stop eating. Nibble haphazardly on the edge of a bagel, then squish the rest into a glass of milk. Watch it bloat. Pour out the orange juice and drink a second cup of coffee. Then a third. When hungry, have a diet coke. The carbonation fills you up, and the caffeine gives you energy. Stay awake nights. Wait.

Ditch AP English and visit Planned Parenthood, the downtown branch. At ten a.m. the waiting room's already filled up, so when you open the door you're hit with a blast of hot, sticky air. Everyone turns to look, then turns back to their conversations. It's a friendly scene, mostly Latina women in their thirties and forties talking in Spanish while their children run circles around them. They all look settled in, like they've been there for hours. Sign in on an old clipboard and sit down in the last empty chair. You're the only teenager; everyone else is in class.

Wait. Stare at the walls. A few announcements are tacked up near the front, one an orange warning about the above-average radioactivity detected in the area. Below it are scratched-up plastic holders with pamphlets on STDs, pregnancy, proper condom use—the same ones a thirty-something Planned Parenthood volunteer brought when she spoke to your health class last month. "What's most important is that you plan ahead," she said, then told a story about how the week before she was in this very unprepared situation with a guy she'd started seeing. "We were like, 'What do you want to do?' and I was thinking, 'I should know better, I teach this stuff!'" The main message she got across was that she had a new boyfriend.

When the woman at the sign-in window calls your name, she's already looking straight at you. Walk up and say, "I'd like a pregnancy test," clearly and firmly, the way you practiced in your head. She buzzes you through the door. She hands you a styrofoam cup and points you to the bathroom. Pee in the cup. The cup has no lid. Walk back through the hall and hand the cup to the woman.

In five minutes, another woman calls you back into a cramped clinic room. She closes the door. "So, do you know what you want to do?" she says.

Ask how much abortions cost. In Los Angeles, the government pays for contraceptives, pelvic exams, and HIV tests if you're a high school student. If you want a free abortion though, you have to qualify for Medicare or Medicaid. "In any case, you have to be at least eight weeks pregnant to get an abortion here," she says. She recommends another clinic that does it at six weeks. "Plus they're cheaper," she says. "$160."

She hands you a proof of pregnancy form, a photocopied half-sheet with a checkmark next to "pregnant." "Don't lose it, you'll need it for the abortion," she says, "and don't forget to make an appointment with the clinic." She gives you a buck-up smile. Nod the way you do when your calculus teacher explains a concept then stares hard at the class for signs of understanding. Fold the sheet and stick it in your backpack.

Walk up two blocks to take the Melrose bus to your afternoon classes. All the seats on the bus are taken. Grab onto a pole and watch the buildings go by: All American Party Store, Paramount Pictures, squat white shops with thick prison bars on the windows and signs that say just LIQUOR. The streets get cleaner as you go west, then dirty again in front of the school. Before getting off the bus, scribble yourself a note about being sick, then fake your mom's signature under it. When you get to the door though, the teacher on duty doesn't see you because she's laughing with a trio of her students. "I mean, one was a flat and one had a heel, like two inches!" she says. "I thought it felt funny but I still didn't realize it until second period!" One of the students—a guy in your French class—sees you and slyly cocks his head to the left, a signal to sneak in, fast. As you do he laughs loudly, putting his arm on the teacher's shoulder and turning his body to block you from view.

———

After school, call the clinic. It's called Family Planning Associates Medical Group, according to the recording while you're on hold. Wait. When the receptionist answers, she takes your name and gives you a Saturday morning appointment. She tells you not to eat for twelve hours before the abortion, "or you may not wake up, okay?" She says this very firmly then waits for you to say okay before going on. She's used to talking to teenagers. She instructs you to bring a driver for the ride home. Ask, "What about the bus?" "No," she says. "Girl, you need a driver."

Call Ryan that night, after he gets home from his part-time job delivering pizzas. Without preamble, say, "So, I'm calling because, I'm pregnant." Hear him suck in air. He says, "Can you hold on for a minute?" Then there's silence. When he comes back on the line he says, "Hey." Then there's silence again.

Let the silence stretch. There's a part of you that's excited to be having this conversation, that's proud in a way to have surprised him, to know more than he does. Before this he hadn't called you for a little over a week, and you'd begun to suspect he wasn't planning to call at all. When he first heard your voice on the phone, he probably thought you'd come up with some coy excuse to hear his voice. Now you have his attention.

Not that you and Ryan ever talked much, on the phone or off. You met him at a party Monica threw when her parents were out of town. He was a quiet one, but he was cute and tall and had a car, and the girls hung around him, so the guys did too. He was the exact kind of guy that never went for you, but halfway through the party suddenly the two of you were sitting on the front steps together, haloed by the bright porch light. You talked vaguely about the people at the party; you didn't really know anyone in common. At some point he said he lived with his mom, like you.

You made out with him behind the house for hours, first standing against the wall until your neck hurt—he's a foot taller than you—then sitting twistedly on the concrete. He gave you hickeys, hideously big purple ones. You gave him a blow job, but stopped before he came because you thought you heard someone coming around the house. He said he'd break up with his girlfriend, and the next week, you heard from Monica who heard from Laney that he had indeed dumped her, a Waspy brunette called Jenny.

Those were the happy times, when you got the news about each other through the grapevine. Once you started talking directly, things turned shitty.

"Are you okay?" he says now. Answer with the abortion appointment info. Say, "I think that's what we should do." "Yeah," he says quickly, "I'm way too young to have a baby." His voice turns to a whisper, so you know his mom's home. It's almost eleven so soon she'll yell at him to get off the phone. He quickly agrees to split the cost. Give him the appointment info again; it's in eleven days. Tell him to honk when he gets to your place so you can just run out. Tell him he can't be late this time.

———————————

Each day, follow the regular schedule of classes. Marvel at how normal everything seems, how unchanged. The steady part of you, the part that memorizes ten SAT vocab words a night and recalculates the problems you got wrong on the physics test, has kicked in. There's no room to panic. It's just about following procedure: Get pregnancy test, make appointment, find ride, abort fetus.

On Wednesday morning, get what looks like your period, except a darker, almost brownish red and a thicker texture than usual. Be surprised. Put a pad on. After school, go to Monica's. Her dad's a gynecologist. Tell her the situation. "Oh no," she says, but sounds a bit excited. She's a virgin. She says you should call her dad at work. You've met him dozens of times, but she says she'll tell him you're "a friend" and he won't know who you are. Agree to this, then take the phone.

Her dad's voice is shaky, like he knows he's doing something wrong, giving you advice over the phone. He says maybe you're miscarrying, maybe you're not. There are these things called false miscarriages, like false labors, he explains. Hang up and call Planned Parenthood for a second opinion. The Santa Monica office says call an ambulance immediately. The downtown office says wait it out—it's probably nothing.

Wait it out.

Wonder which time the pregnancy happened. Count days. Decide it was probably on the night in Venice. Ryan suggested going to the beach and it sounded romantic, but when you got there it was close to eleven, so the beach was closed. You started making out. His car was a small two-door, and instead of getting in the backseat he liked to recline the passenger seat and get on top of you. He'd brought a condom but he started putting it on inside out, which ruined it. "I can pull out," he said hopefully, and he did, but barely, coming on your vagina instead of in it. He had a little pack of tissues and as you cleaned up you noticed there was a man outside, leaning against a yellow pole at the edge of the parking lot, looking your way. "Is that guy watching us?" you said, and Ryan turned to look. "Weirdo," he said, and zipped up. You looked at the man again and he looked right back at you, hard. "Is he trying to tell us something?" you said. "No," Ryan said. "He's just getting off watching us. Perv."

Get stomach cramps and curl up in the fetal position on Monica's bed. She curls up next to you and holds your hand. The gesture feels fake somehow, like the two of you are posing for a film about the perils of unprotected sex.

Go home and pull off the pad and dig your fingers through the clumps of blood for the semblance of a child. Find none. Throw it away, then wish you had searched harder, ripped it apart.

Since you could still be pregnant, don't let the first trimester pass you by. Monica says even if you've miscarried, they probably need to scrape out your womb. She's heard about it somewhere. Decide to keep the appointment.

On Saturday Ryan arrives fifteen minutes late. "I had to run errands for my mom," he says, and sounds more defensive than sorry. The clinic accepts only money orders, so you stop at Bank of America for your eighty dollars, at Wells Fargo for his eighty dollars, then at Ralph's, the busy one on Third and Vermont, to buy the money order. Get lost on the way to the clinic and argue about directions. He tries his way, then yours. You're right, of course; you have the Thomas Guide on your lap. When you arrive you're twenty minutes late, angry, and panicked.

Family Planning Associates is newer and cleaner than expected. Inside the front door is a lobby-like area with no one in it. Ryan spins around a few times studying the room, like he's making sure it's empty. The office, he reads on a sign as you're about to knock on a door, is in the basement. He leads the way down.

Three people are waiting in the long office. Its windowless walls are a pale, creamy yellow, the cushioned chairs fake black leather. The receptionist sits in a movie ticket booth–like office. Sign in and hand her your pregnancy test slip through the semicircle at the base of the plastic window.

Wait. Think about the short blurb you read in *Glamour* last year, the one about a girl who went to get an abortion with a boyfriend. When her name was called she turned to him and said, "I don't want to do this," and he said, "I don't want to either." So they left the clinic and got married. That was one of a half dozen letters from readers about how they'd met their soul mates. You think about this story not because you don't want to have an abortion—you most definitely do—but you wish it wasn't this way, with someone you only communicate with through appointment times.

Wonder what he talked about with his ex-girlfriend. Did they have conversations about music and school and love? You talk about none of those things, though you thought you might, when you first met him. But you saw he lived in a modest little bungalow house in West LA, a mansion compared to the dank, cramped walk-up apartment in Koreatown you lived in with your sister and your mom, who was never around, and who when she was, you wished she wasn't, answering the phone with "Who is talking?" in her aggressive accent, arranging in cheap plastic vases the discards from her job at the discount flower shop, the one next to the dollar store. So you kept a no-nonsense exterior, nothing could hurt you, there was nothing you hadn't seen or done before. "Are you sleeping with anyone else?" You asked one afternoon when he was driving you back home, asked it like it didn't matter, like you were asking for practical reasons, since you only used condoms sporadically. "What?" he said, then, "No." He drove on for a while, then said, "Are you?" He had this bemused look on his face, like he'd agreed to play a game you'd invented, but there was a thin pallor of fear under it too.

Out of the corner of your eye you see a guy walking down the hall toward you, and when you turn to look, you see it's Sam, a guy in your AP English class. When he sees you he literally covers his face with his hand and ducks into the closest open door. You're less embarrassed than surprised to see him there; he's a big, awkward, lumbering type and doesn't have a girlfriend. "Do you know him?" Ryan asks. Shrug. Say, "He's in one of my classes."

After a few minutes, the receptionist calls your name and hands you a stack of sheets, the top one titled Elective Abortion. To put it quite simply, the contents of the uterus are removed by suction, by a machine that operates under the same principles as a vacuum cleaner, it begins. Start skimming. Perforation . . .

Cervical Laceration . . . Failure to Terminate Pregnancy (Rarely, estimated about one in 2,000 cases . . .). Ryan reads along with you, but you read faster than he does, flip the page before he's done. Sign the papers.

The receptionist directs you through a door and as you leave Ryan gets up, looks like he's about to say something, but then just stands there. Give him a wave.

You're taken to a small office where a middle-aged woman starts going over the important details in the sheets; it's assumed no one reads them with care. "For two weeks after the abortion, don't put anything in your vagina," she says. "No sex, no douche, no tampons." She takes your money order. "This covers emergency services if something goes wrong," she says, "including hospitalization, but not medication." She makes a wry face at that last part. "There's a twenty-four-hour 800 number and around-the-clock assistance." She's a firm, no-nonsense type, making eye contact after each point and waiting for you to nod before going on. Nod emphatically. Wonder if you look English-illiterate.

She hands you a styrofoam cup, this time with your name on it. This clinic's bathroom is nicer, chrome and fake marble with a rectangular hole in the wall where you deposit the cup. Through it, you see what looks like a lab. As you squat to pee, you see a male hand take the cup that's already sitting at the hole's ledge. Place your cup in its stead.

Outside, a different woman gives you a locker key on a wristband, the kind that looks like a circular telephone cord. Then she hands you a blue outfit to wear for the procedure, complete with thin blue plastic pouches with elasticized ankles for footwear. "The opening should be in the back," she says. She points to a door. "Go in there when you're ready," she says, and leaves.

Step into the closet-sized locker and change, then go through the designated door, one poufy step at a time. The room's packed with thirty or so other girls, all like Smurfettes in their blue robes, and as you sit, someone yells out your name. It's Helen, a girl in your chemistry class. "Oh my god," she says, "we're both here!" The girl next to Helen giggles. "Oh, you guys know each other?" Smile back at both of them. Helen's had the same boyfriend for the last two years; he takes the same bus you do, gets on and off three stops closer to school. Sam must be Helen's ride.

The room quiets down again. Wait. After fifteen minutes, ask the overweight girl next to you how many girls go in at a time. She shakes her head, then turns back to her *Cosmopolitan*. Notice her eyes are swollen.

A woman in pink and purple scrubs comes in, holding a clipboard. She calls your name tentatively, like she's apologizing. Raise your hand. She gestures for you to come out into the hall. Shuffle out. She has your proof of pregnancy form in one hand and something square in the other. The square has a blue minus on it. "I'm not sure what happened," she says, "but you're not pregnant anymore." Nod. Say, "I thought maybe I was miscarrying." She relaxes, gives you back the money order. Ask, "Do I need to—do anything?" She shakes her head. "You're free to leave," she says, then gives you a big congratulatory smile.

Change back into your clothes and put the robe and shoes next to the trash can, which is already overflowing. In the waiting room, Ryan's deep into a football game. When you call his name, he startles, then rushes over. "What happened?" he says. Say, "I miscarried." "What?" he says.

Turn around and start up the stairs. He'll follow.

It's still sunny outside. In the car, say, "I got the money order back." He nods. You've forgotten where you put it, and after emptying out the purse, you find it in the pocket of your jeans. Cross out Family Planning Associates on the Pay To line and replace it with his name, acknowledging the change with a signature. "The bank won't take that," he says. Argue about banking procedures. Say, "If it doesn't go through, call me, and I'll just pay for it." "That's not what I meant," he says.

Realize he's driven all the way down Third Street into Koreatown, long past the Wells Fargo branch you stopped at earlier. Now he can't find another Wells Fargo. Pass three Bank of Americas looking for one until he stops at a residential area and asks a dog walker in red for directions. When he follows them, you spot the bank. The ATM line is long. Wait.

Watch him weary in line. A woman in a gray business suit keeps changing her mind, pulling out transaction slips and her card before reinserting it and starting over. When he's finally at the machine, he takes a while, hitting the wrong buttons. He comes back with four twenties. His hands are sweaty when he hands you the money. He asks if you want to go to the bank now. Say no.

When he pulls up in front of your apartment, say bye opening the car door, without looking at him. "Bye," he says. Walk down the narrow alley, turn left to go up the stairs. He's still there; you can hear the engine of his old Ford Fiesta, running hoarsely.

Don't turn to look. You don't know it now but you'll see him again, when you call him three weeks later. "Just checking to see how you're doing," you'll say in your best casual voice. You'll go out to watch *Batman Returns*, then have sex in his car on the third floor of the parking lot of the Beverly Connection. It'll be a lot like the first time, quick and furtive and uncomfortable, though this time, you'll use a condom. Afterwards he'll hold the door on his side ajar and drop the used thing on the concrete with a soft plop. He'll do this casually, almost confidently, without comment. For a minute it'll feel vaguely like you're both just following a script, acting out a long-ingrained habit you never knew you had.

Cake Time

I met Ben the day I moved off-campus, into Carrie's spare bed-room. Carrie was a girl from my music appreciation class. She had beautiful, dark brown eyes, though it was hard to notice them; she hid behind a scrim of mousy hair and soft chub, which gave her the sodden air of someone who'd found a tenuous contentment on Paxil. Her pale olive skin hinted at Greek ancestry. She was technically a townie; her mom worked in the college's printing department, so Carrie got to attend tuition-free.

I was on scholarship, which was the sole reason for my staying at this no-name liberal arts school in rural Pennsylvania. Our two-bedroom apartment had a tract housing feel with cheap, greenish carpeting that pilled and faintly stained my socks. The walls looked like they'd been repainted fairly recently but poorly so; clumps of rubbery paint clotted under the windowsills.

I was breaking down a cardboard box when Carrie knocked on the open door. Ben was standing behind her. He didn't wait to be introduced.

"Whatever she's told you, they're all lies," he said, taking my hand in a grand, debonair gesture, then shaking it with a cocky smile. He was, admittedly, a good-looking guy. He looked to be in his late twenties; he had an adult rakishness about him that agitated me. You could tell he was Carrie's brother—they had the same dark hair and liquid eyes—but he was close to six feet tall, lean without looking skinny.

"I didn't know you had a brother," I said to Carrie. My voice came out in an excited, lilting tone, which made me flush.

Carrie turned to Ben. "She just moved in."

Ben shrugged. He asked me what my major was, and when I said English, jauntily offered his opinion that English was a catchall major for people who didn't know what to do with their lives. Then he winked. I asked him what he'd majored in.

"I studied economics for a while," he said. "But I left. In business, you need real life experience more than book smarts."

"So what do you do now?" I asked. The phone rang then, and Carrie went to get it.

"Internet startup." He put on his shit-eating grin again. "Top secret. I could tell you, but then I'd have to kill you."

"Really," I said. "Good luck with that." By this time I'd managed to bring my high-pitched tone under control, and my words sounded more sarcastic than I'd intended. He opened his mouth into a look of surprise, then closed it for a grimace. I tried to think of something smart and ingratiating to say, but the moment tensed then tore, leaving each of us with a jagged half.

"It's Mom," Carrie called from the living room. "She wants to talk to you."

He went to get the phone, then left without saying goodbye. After that he didn't bother to make conversation when he came around, just gave me a disparaging nod of acknowledgement when he saw me, before turning his attention back to Carrie.

But I learned plenty about Ben anyway. Carrie had a high opinion of him, though I gathered that he basically just worked at the Dairy Queen, where his girlfriend Marcy also worked, and spent his nights drinking beer with his friends. Whenever Carrie and I talked I felt like she was feeling over my brain in search of a crack, then on finding one, scrabbling in her fingernails. "He looks out for me," she said, her eyes drifting up moonily. "He doesn't want me dating the losers around here, even the ones at college, because they're all from hick towns too. Right?" There was a desperation in her eyes as she asked this that grated against her usual flaccid expression. She said that since she'd turned sixteen he let her drink at his parties. "Just one drink though, so I don't get in any trouble." I could imagine Carrie at these events, in a dingy house like our own, nursing her warm beer quietly in a corner until the pretty girls left and Ben's friends noticed her as an easy target. Maybe it was a good thing Ben kept her under his thumb after all.

I asked her if any of Ben's friends were cute, if she had dated any of them, and she shook her head confusedly, like the idea had never occurred to her. I wondered if she was a virgin. I wondered if she thought I was. I imagine she thought me bookish and naïve, since she didn't spend enough time on campus to know anything different.

In fact I'd screwed things up there starting the first week of my freshman year, when I'd met Allen, an upperclassman who'd had a way of making me feel like the urbane, provocative woman I'd wanted to be. He'd also had a girlfriend at another school. When I met her at a party I told her, "You're so lucky, Allen's a great guy," before getting drunk and yelling from outside his door about how he was doing to her what he'd done to me last week. "You have a lot of nerve, calling here after the shit you pulled last night," he'd said the last time I'd called him. "And we're gonna be fine, so fuck you."

After that I'd spent most of my time drinking and hooking up indiscriminately, my living exhibition piece to show how little I cared. I'd tried out bad ideas, and when they didn't work, tried them harder. Eventually, when my friends started seriously dating the guys that had humiliated me, I'd determined to disappear from campus.

And I had, more or less. Now a junior, I stayed in the apartment except to attend classes, most of them evening seminars that I'd trudge into in a soporific haze, staking out my usual corner seat a few minutes early. The other students would come in in an energetic patter, bounding up the stairs then reconfiguring their gaits to walk in the room with cheerful, attenuated steps. Their expressions seemed always to be holding back a mix of mirth and mockery that in my more paranoid moments seemed to be masking a rumor about me. At these times I felt an indeterminate sense of revulsion and shame.

After class I'd go rejoin Carrie on the couch, who sat with the TV on, wearing a glazed expression and an ill-fitting T-shirt, watching sitcom reruns while haphazardly negotiating her homework. I began to notice her little study habits, the laborious attention with which she formed her tidy block letters, the indiscriminate way she dragged her highlighter over her books, so that in the end, almost every line of text was painted a fluorescent blue. I got the sense she didn't do well in her classes. Most nights I dozed next to her until she patted me on the shoulder, waking me to tell me to get to bed.

The days shuffled on this way until Carrie's twenty-first birthday that March. For the occasion, Ben organized to take her—and by extension, me—to a local dive known as The Pub, one of the two bars in town. I knew it would be just me and the townies, but I felt vaguely excited in spite of myself; it had been that long since I'd had a night out.

Carrie too seemed in high spirits. "It's my night," she kept saying, plucking and painting herself at the bathroom sink. Her inexpert but dogged manner reminded me of a nurse-in-training repeatedly trying to finagle a needle into a slippery vein. Though she still wore her usual T-shirt-and-jeans combo, she'd dressed to stick out—the denim low enough to show the gentle fat of her midriff, the red top a tight low V-neck. She put on a garish lipstick to match and kept checking her teeth for smears.

Ben honked from the curb right on time, at nine. The pale blue paint of his car was rusting at the edges. Ben's girlfriend Marcy sat in the front seat. "Nice to meet you," she said, turning to shake my hand in an awkward fingers-only squeeze. I guessed she was about my age, though she had primped to look older. She wore harsh black eyeliner that made her blue eyes look surreal, like they were on a different plane from the rest of her face. The damaged ends of her bleached hair frizzed out around her face in a halo of blond cotton candy. The car was suffused with the scent of her soft, musky perfume.

Ben gave me his usual nod. "Always a pleasure," he added this time. Then he saw Carrie and did a double take. He started driving, keeping his hand on the gear shift, and at the first turn, Marcy softly placed her hand on top of his, her long, violet fingernails gleaming under the streetlights. The gesture seemed oddly sensual and illicit, creating a subtle charge that silenced the car until we parked.

The Pub was a longish, windowless room with cheap wood-paneled walls, a no-frills bar positioned at one end. The place was still mostly empty. A few people stood around holding their beers in squat, dissatisfied postures. Three shaky-looking men sat in a row at the bar.

"Mickey," Ben yelled. "It's my sister's twenty-first birthday!"

The bartender Mickey waved, then lined up a dozen or so shot glasses and started pouring tequila. I joined the first round, then asked for a rum and coke. "For Carrie's friend, anything," Mickey said, with a gallant bow that made me giggle. He was cute, about Ben's age, maybe a little older. When he set down the drink he smiled, revealing a silver glint. I slunk back toward Carrie.

"He has a girlfriend," Ben said, with a sardonic leer.

"And a metal tooth," I said.

Ben shook his head like he was exasperated, then signaled Mickey for another round. Carrie reached for another shot. "Take it easy," Ben said, grabbing her arm. "Pace yourself."

Carrie uncharacteristically hardened her face. "It's my night," she said, then grabbed a shot and took it, her eyes fixed on Ben. Her look was defiant, if slightly tinged with fear.

For a second Ben looked like he was going to start yelling. But he relaxed and laughed. "Damn right, it's your night," he said, thumping her back once, rather hard, with his palm.

The night sped up. The bar filled and morphed into a glitter of glass and ice and amber liquids. People shifted subtly to reveal their fey, glamorous sides. I started to appreciate the small, hopeful efforts that had been put into the night—a gangly brunette's blowout, the smart crease in a short guy's khakis, Carrie's impasto lipstick. I noticed Marcy, the way she stood displaying her nails against her glass of ice cubes, tense and taut in her tiny skirt and scuffed strappy heels as if she was en pointe, standing at the ready for some cue from Ben. She had long, thin appendages and a waistless middle. Once in a while she joined the conversation by saying, "That's interesting," followed by a small, knowing smile, belied by her uncertain eyes. That uncertainty reminded me of Carrie, her expression when she'd asked if I thought it was normal that Ben called every night for a rundown of her day. I said I wasn't a good person to ask; I didn't have a brother.

Ben seemed to know everyone who came in; I introduced myself to some of them. "So you're Carrie's roommate," they each said. A heavy guy boasted he was Ben's best friend. "Are you working on the Internet startup with Ben?" I asked. "Start-up?" he said, then snickered. "Oh, the shoe store thing." He said he worked for the city, trimming trees. I said something inane about how great it must be to work outside, and he nodded embarrassedly, perhaps for me.

Suddenly I heard my name. It was Anne, my roommate from freshman year. "I haven't seen you all semester!" she yelled, spitting a little. "I called your number in the phone book and the girl who answered said I had the wrong number. I thought maybe you'd transferred!"

"Still here," I said, plastering a grin. "I moved off campus."

"I missed you!" she said. She lunged in for a hug. She was drunk, but this warmed me to her. We guzzled the drinks in our hands, talking in slurry exclamations. "You know Jillian transferred?" Anne said. "Or dropped out more like?"

Jillian was another girl from our floor, the baby-faced one at the end of the hall. I shook my head. Anne said Jillian broke her hip when a drunk linebacker who was fucking her in the bathroom at Phi Delt dropped her against the urinal. Her scream was so loud people at the party rushed in and saw her, her shirt and bra scrunched up at her armpits, her bare ass on the urine-spattered floor. It was a while before the ambulance came.

"That snobby cow," Anne said, then cackled maliciously. "That was mean, right?"

We laughed. I offered to get us more drinks. "On me," I said.

It was crowded at the bar, but I squeezed through. "Mickey!" I yelled. "Two more!" He nodded affably and started making them. A couple people who'd been waiting turned to look at me with curiosity and loathing. I didn't care. My mind swam; I drummed my fingers against the bar wantonly. Smiling, I looked around, then startled. Allen was at my right, sneering. Our shoulders were pressed together.

"So you're fucking townies now?" he said, pointing his chin at Mickey.

At that my heart started thudding in my skull. Allen's face turned into a violent blur. I turned toward where Mickey was making the drinks. I remembered the last time I'd slept with Allen, at his fraternity's end-of-year party, months after that final phone call. After getting drunk in the basement, I'd snuck up into his room. He was alone, studying for his sociology final. I said I'd heard he and his girlfriend had broken up. I stumbled over him. "Do you realize how pathetic you are?" he'd said, taking off my clothes.

The drinks came. I picked them up and walked away, focused on staying balanced.

Carrie was talking to some of Ben's friends. I joined her circle but was too jittery to follow the conversation. I glanced around the bar; every sideways glance I got back seemed stained with disgust and pity. I saw Ben and could tell he wanted to leave too. He was studying the college students with a defensive sneer. "These fucking kids," he said. "They don't know how to drink."

"We should go," I said. "Take the party home. Cake time."

"I want cake!" Carrie said. I saw across the bar that Anne had found the girls she'd arrived with, her sorority sisters. They gesticulated energetically to communicate over the noise of the crowd.

Exiting the bar was like entering another world, an eerie silence amplified by the glow of a lone streetlight. During the quick drive home Ben seemed preoccupied, but once back at the house we were united by our effort to have a good time. I helped him unload the party stuff from the trunk, then we created a mini assembly line in the kitchen, me chipping apart the ice cubes to put in the red plastic cups, Ben filling them with equal parts Bacardi and Coke. Marcy cut generous slices of supermarket sheet cake onto paper plates. Carrie tuned the radio to a top 40 station, and we started drinking in earnest.

"To Carrie," Ben said.

"To me!" Carrie said. She was a happy drunk, if slightly belligerent. She commanded us to dance and we did, bopping to a new hip-hop track none of us had heard before. After a while of this, a slow love song came on. I plopped down on the couch and took some gulps from my drink. Ben grabbed Marcy and started slow dancing. Carrie kept gyrating on her own for a while off rhythm, then gave up and sat down too.

By this time it must have been around two in the morning. My drunkenness was settling into a lethargic buzz. We watched Ben and Marcy dance. Ben started putting on a show. He pulled Marcy in really tight so their whole bodies were pressed against each other, making it hard for them to move. Then he started kissing her. Marcy complied, miming passion.

"Get a room," Carrie said.

Ben seemed to relent, sitting down on the couch and pulling Marcy down to sit next to him. But then he started kissing her again. The song droned on to its third verse. As it ended Ben snuck another glance at us before sliding his hand down to one of Marcy's breasts, rubbing his palm over it, then squeezing it.

"Just fuck in front of us, why don't you," Carrie said.

"Yeah, seriously," I said.

Ben looked up. "If you don't want to see it, don't look," he said. Then he jammed his face into the crook of Marcy's neck. Marcy closed her eyes and tilted her head back affectedly.

Carrie and I looked at each other, then burst out laughing. Then Carrie got an impish gleam in her eye. "No, we mean it," she said. "Do it."

Ben and Marcy kept kissing.

"Do it, do it," Carrie said in a rhythmic chant. She looked at me, nodding, and I joined her. "Do it, do it, do it."

He shifted his eyes to look at us, his mouth stuck on Marcy's. We kept chanting. "Do it, do it, do it, do it . . ." We watched his expression morph, going from puzzled to questioning to scared, his hands groping about Marcy's body aimlessly, until our chorus lost its energy and faded out. Carrie picked up her drink, took a big gulp, then turned to me. "He's always all talk," she said loudly.

I snorted. "Pathetic," I said.

Ben acted like he didn't hear us, but I saw his jaw set. Suddenly he started kissing Marcy more aggressively. He unbuttoned her shirt, then pushed it off her shoulders to reveal a beige bra, a thick, padded polyester thing with cups that looked like they could stand up on their own. At this, Carrie and I got quiet. The radio was playing a Matchbox Twenty song. Marcy's body turned rigid but didn't make any move to stop him. He unlatched the bra, then as he took it off glanced over at us to make sure if we were watching. We were. He pushed Marcy on her back, and at this Marcy put her left arm over her breasts, hiding them. While leaning over and kissing her, he put his hands under her skirt and started taking off her panties. They were a basic cotton pair with a daisy print and blue elastic trimming, the kind a kid would wear. Marcy had her face turned away, toward the back of the couch, her eyes closed in an expression simulating sexual concentration. Ben then positioned himself between her legs, got up on his knees, then unzipped his pants and took out his erect penis. He stroked it, peeking at us again, this time with a look that seemed somewhat shy, like he was seeking our approval.

The radio was now playing a Shania Twain song. Ben lay down on top of Marcy and appeared to enter her, though I couldn't see; the skirt was in the way. Once he started thrusting, Marcy's body seemed to go limp, like she'd passed out. He kept going at it somewhat alone, then clutched Marcy's hair near her scalp, pulling it roughly. At this she started emitting small, squeaky moans to his rhythm, like a squeeze toy. He started fucking her harder. He balanced himself up on one hand and played with the waist of Marcy's skirt, eventually sliding it off; it was a wraparound. When he did that Marcy bent her legs and with her feet pushed off Ben's pants and boxers. He helped by wiggling until they were half way down his thighs. Then he pushed Marcy's right leg so it was hanging down over the couch, and tilted their bodies so that we could get a better look at his penis moving in and out of her. She had reddish pubic hair.

They went at it steadily in this position for a while, long enough to feel anticlimactic. Eventually Marcy's protective arm dropped off to dangle off the side of the couch. I noticed that one of her breasts was significantly bigger than the other. Finally Ben grunted, then sat up while simultaneously pulling up his pants. He zipped up, then looked at us. His expression was dazed and anxious, like he didn't know what had just happened.

"Cover me," Marcy said in a whiny tone. She looked sleepy with a sheen of sweat, as if she'd just woken up from a bad dream. Ben put his forearm over her pubic hair. He leaned over her body and with his other hand started picking up Marcy's clothes from the floor and placing them on her chest. Once he'd accomplished this, the two started working together to get Marcy dressed, using weird, cumbersome movements that attempted to shield her nakedness. Then they sat side by side on the couch, meekly, hands on their laps.

Bon Jovi came on the radio. "I hate this song," Carrie said, then stumbled over to change the station. She found a rock station with a thrumming beat. She made a raise the roof gesture. "Get up," she said.

"Hey, it's not your birthday anymore." Ben said. He reached for his drink.

"It's still her party," I said. I poured more rum into Carrie's and my cups, though they were still mostly full. I drank some then got up and danced with her.

The night returned to its former disheveled revelry, all of us dancing and drinking again. At a certain point Marcy said she thought she was going to puke and I went outside with her, rubbed her back while she took some deep breaths. For a moment I held her wrist; its pulse quivered and twitched, like a feather stuck in a revolving door.

Eventually I must have dozed off on the couch, because Carrie patted me awake. "You'll feel better if you sleep in bed," she said. The music had been turned off and her face looked saintly and luminous, framed by the light of the floor lamp and the quiet of early morning. When I sat up I saw Ben and Marcy collecting cups and plates in a careful, inefficient manner, awkwardly holding a gauzy trash bag between them. "Leave it, I'll get it in the morning," I murmured, and staggered off to bed.

The next day, after I finally woke up, I sat at the dining table with my coffee, focused on the vacant throbbing in my head. The familiarity of the sensation was oddly comforting, almost pleasurable. It was a little after ten, and the sun cut through the windows, slicing the room with bands of light, suffusing my body with a sharp, benevolent heat. I heard small, shuffling noises from Carrie's room; I imagined her still in her red T-shirt and jeans, her face runny with makeup and bloated from last night's alcohol.

But when she came out, she looked as she did every morning, sleepy but well-rested. "Is there coffee left?" she asked, and when I nodded, said "All right!" and went into the kitchen to get a cup.

When Carrie sat down to join me I had my eyes closed, slowly turning my head from side to side to stop the ringing in my ears. I was trying to recreate the feelings I'd had the first time Allen and I slept together, when afterwards we giggled like co-conspirators, hiding under the comforter while his roommates came in, banging around looking for a basketball. But this time I could only remember Allen's expression at the bar, his contorted lip and grimace, the ugly, taunting voice that somehow seemed more like mine than his. I remembered my shock at this change in him, but couldn't relive that sensation either. All my memories felt dulled and flattened, like I was watching them via a faraway screen, the sound on mute.

"Hey, wake up," Carrie said. "Seriously, you sleep way too much." I opened my eyes. She blew on her coffee before sipping it; she'd added a creamer that smelled synthetic and luxurious. As she drank she caught me up on what I'd missed after I'd fallen asleep, which was that Ben and Marcy had apologized right before leaving. "I was actually feeling kind of bad, like we forced them into it. But when they sobered up they were like, 'Sorry, we were really drunk.' So I was like, 'It's okay, don't worry about it.'"

"Really?" I said. I thought about Marcy's ragdoll postures, the way she turned her face away, almost burying it from view, the way she let Ben tilt her pelvis toward us, pressing her leg down off the couch as if the appendage didn't even belong to her. I remembered her one self-protective gesture, how she kept covering her breasts with her arm, right up until the end. The feeling behind the gesture seemed oddly familiar to me, though I couldn't remember ever taking it on.

The Supplies

The temp agency was on the sixth floor of a tall glass building that looked glossy, almost glamorous from the outside. But the one-room office itself was dingy, crammed with metal desks and chipped veneer counters, vaguely demarcated with gray partition walls. I was made to wait sitting against one of these for half an hour until I was called before Lisa, a slender woman with thin, tense lips that clashed with her expressionless forehead, probably Botoxed. She looked to be in her early forties, two decades older than me. She wore an expensive gray skirt suit that seemed wasted in the cramped office, which employed just two other women, a receptionist who kept adjusting her wig and a nervous girl who rushed back and forth, making photocopies.

Lisa glanced at my résumé then studied me with more care, her eyes pausing over the unironed legs of my pants. She said that her office really handled only administrative, data entry type jobs. I said that was exactly what I was looking for. She pursed her lips. I said ten dollars an hour was all I expected. She looked unconvinced but assigned me a battery of tests.

I was great at typing and getting around Microsoft Word, but was made to retake the data entry and Excel assessments until my scores were deemed adequate.

When I left, it was mid-afternoon. There was a Whole Foods across the street; I went in and picked out "natural" Oreos. I opened the package while walking to the car and ate as I drove home. Then I got back into bed and unpaused the *Dexter* episode streaming on Netflix. "But it's not that simple," Dexter said. "I have a code. Rules. Responsibilities."

I'd seen all the episodes before, but rewatching them, I felt a predictable, wallowing comfort.

I hadn't always been this way. Until a month ago, I'd done just fine at a new tech company that did IT work for all the internet startups popping up. Basically, I was an assistant there, but after learning I was an English major, my bosses—three MBA grads from UCLA—slapped me with the title Corporate Communications Manager and had me write copy for their website, which I cribbed from other websites. This title was why Lisa thought me overqualified. When the company went belly up in the dot-com crash, I thought I'd try freelance writing. But on my own, I fell into a funk. I woke up at five in the morning one day, two in the afternoon the next. I ate junk food. It was tough to get motivated, and tough to find gigs. I picked up just a trickle of assignments, churning out rewrites of press releases for soft news websites. I started to fantasize about menial jobs. I wanted to file, photocopy, and collate, to stick neatly typed labels on folders before alphabetizing them by last name in long, metal file cabinets, even to spend quiet afternoons segregating paper clips by size. That's how I'd found myself at the temp agency.

The next day, Lisa called mid-morning with my first job, a one-day gig at a law office in West Los Angeles that needed an assistant to come in immediately. "It's a traditional firm," Lisa said, "so what you wore when you interviewed here—something like that would be fine." I said I could be there in an hour; she said she'd tell them two, then hung up. I mussed around the bed for that interview outfit and found the pants wedged between the sheets.

Lisa was right; I hurried but still got there at the two-hour mark. The job was in the billing department. A mousy girl about my age gave me two stacks of papers; I was to match the check stubs with the invoices. I don't think I really helped much; most of the stubs had little identifying information, so I kept having to ask the girl for help. The actual task too seemed pointless, circular; I asked the girl what happened to the paired papers and she shrugged and pointed to a file cabinet. It stood big and pristine in its corner, like a readymade in a museum. "No one ever looks in there," she said. She seemed to like me though; perhaps she liked having an underling, or was lonely. At the end of the day she said if it were up to her, I'd be hired full-time. The department really needed to make this a permanent position, she said, then signed and faxed my timesheet for me.

My second job was at the small management office of a high-rise office building in El Segundo. It was a two-day gig, ten to three each day. I validated parking tickets and transferred the occasional phone call to one of the three employees. The manager was a friendly, overweight man. At noon he asked me if I wanted the banana his wife had packed for him; it had freckles, which he found unappetizing. I took it and thanked him. There was little for me to do, the phone calls were so few and far between that I wondered why they didn't just answer their own calls, but when I packed up for the day the manager said, "We really should have someone here full-time. I'll talk to Maira about it in the morning."

Maira was the boss. "I'm not sure," I said the next day, when she asked what my long-term plans were.

"I just don't want someone who's going to leave in six months," she said in a haughty tone. When I said I understood, her eyes widened, then turned hard. She gave me a sharp nod and clicked her heels back into her office.

Lisa called me on my way home. "They'd like you back next week, but I've got a full-time thing for twelve dollars an hour too," she said. "It's an ad agency. Temp-to-hire."

I took it. When I hung up I felt an anxious sort of happiness. Two companies had wanted me. As I drove my mood swung erratically, giddy one moment, then self-satisfied to the point of being sardonic, then flaily and frantic with apprehension.

On Monday I got to the agency a little before nine. The office had a sleek, modern look, like it had recently gone through an expensive remodel. At the reception desk sat an Armenian girl who held her face tilted down under the weight of her heavy high ponytail. She looked sixteen. When I introduced myself she buzzed someone, then kept smiling at me until I turned away to study a well-trimmed fern.

A middle-aged woman called Maureen came out and shook my hand. She asked if I wouldn't mind waiting a bit. "A few fires to put out this morning," she said, wagging her hands around her face, eyebrows raised. I figured I would still get paid. I took a seat on a white leather divan and picked up a copy of *Ad Age*. Less than five minutes later Maureen was hovering over me. "Ready?" she said, grinning.

The job consisted primarily of emailing project drafts to the creative team, then circulating hard copies of the same drafts, though no one looked at the printouts except the copyeditor. I walked through the quiet office dropping papers into plastic in-boxes. The soft, middle-aged geniality of the employees clashed with the sharp image I'd had of creative ad agency types. The women wore busy polyester blouses and skirt suits made with dense, no-iron fabric. Their kids' crayon drawings fidgeted on the cubicle walls. The head writer was a stringy man in his sixties who ran during his lunch break in purple shorts, dodging pedestrians. He tipped an imaginary hat to me whenever I passed his cubicle. Next to him sat the production manager, a heavy woman who drank constantly from a Starbucks cup but still always looked bleary-eyed.

I decided I liked them all, the whole team, in a passive, un-taxing way, though I wondered how they'd been hired, if they'd all come in to their initial interviews with the same fusty clothing and droopy attitudes they displayed now. The only artsy-looking person was the copyeditor, a guy in his mid-thirties called Roy, who had a toned-down Mohawk. He always had his earbuds in; he smiled hazily when he saw me. Maureen said he was newly married. "He got the haircut right after the honeymoon," she confided in a low voice, then asked me to email him to check if black-and-white proofs would do.

To me the office seemed a peaceful place, where I could wallow in its drab, noncompetitive spirit.

When I got home that night I felt calmer than I had in a long time, then the next morning, oddly energized, purposeful. I drank extra coffee and drove to work with an eager, curious attitude. The traffic was unusually light so I arrived a half hour early with a sense that the world had cleared a new path for me. I felt willing, confident. I would beat this junk food habit once and for all. I went into a juice bar on the first floor and ordered a fruit-and-greens smoothie to go. Afterwards, a woman holding a yogurt parfait cup the same way I was holding my smoothie got on the elevator with me. We smiled at each other. I thought positive, encouraging thoughts about the cumulative rewards of diligent work. I felt like I was coming out of a long sleep to join the good people in the world, all with their crucial small roles to play. When the parfait woman got off before me, I said "Have a good day," and she said "You too."

"Well, hello!" Maureen said when she got in, her head bobbing over our shared cubicle wall. "Usually I'm the first one here!"

She gave me more drafts to circulate.

By noon that day, I realized there wasn't much for me to do. Now that I was set up, the job really came down to a couple hours a day. I scuttled about the office trying to look occupied. I stretched things out, drinking glasses of water between tasks, sorting the recycling in the copy room. I spent inordinate amounts of time in the bathroom, sometimes sitting on the toilet, but mostly standing in front of the mirror, picking at my reflection without purpose. Whenever another woman walked in, I gave her a wide grin through the mirror, like I'd been hoping she'd drop by. Usually, the women flashed back equally big, friendly smiles, even the ones that had never met me. Some introduced themselves and we made pleasant, meaningless conversation and inexplicit plans for lunch sometime in the far future. In this way I started some small friendships based on idle gossip. The boss Brian had just bought a Jaguar, I learned, though no one had gotten a summer bonus that year. Roy the copyeditor had called in sick. At first people speculated that he'd gone to Burning Man, but then the news came that he'd gotten his appendix removed.

The day dragged by this way until I finally ended up asking Maureen if there was anything else she needed help with.

Maureen looked up, surprised. "You're so much faster than the last girl!" she said. "We're going to run out of things for you to do!"

I smiled uneasily.

"Let's see here." Maureen turned, eyes scanning about her desk. "Well, everything else is really—I mean, this is really unexpected." She opened her email and started clicking around frantically. "Let's see, let's see." Then she stopped, and looked up at me. "Do you like driving?"

"Driving?" I said blankly, then nodded slowly. "Sure."

"Well it's just that we've got this for Roy," Maureen put her palm on a stack of proofs on her desk, "and this late in the day it'll be hard to get a messenger to go all the way to West Hills. Where do you live?"

"It's okay, I'll go," I said.

"Are you sure? I know it might seem a little—beneath you— but sometimes I deliver proofs too, in a pinch."

"I don't mind, really. I like driving."

"Keep track of the mileage. And just call it a day afterwards. We'll say you were here until six." She winked.

When Roy opened the door his Mohawk was matted and skewed left, giving him the attitude of a truant child woken up from a nap. He was holding an empty CD jewel case. As soon as he saw me he reached to take over the heavy stack of proofs, and in doing so, dropped the case. It bounced on his front step, cracked loudly into two flaps, then bounced again, less tendentiously, to land on the lawn.

"It's okay," he said. "I don't need it."

"Really?" I said. "Okay."

I picked up the pieces and followed him in. The house was airy and furnished with pale, natural wood, spare and blocky, vaguely Japanese. Tinny music played, barely audible. At first I thought it was coming from another room, then realized it was the earbuds, plugged into the laptop on the coffee table. "What are you listening to?" I asked, then wished I hadn't. I probably wouldn't know the band.

Roy set the stack down next to the laptop, then sat down on the couch, carefully, which reminded me about the appendix. He pulled the earbuds out of the laptop and soft, synthesized music came out the speakers. A whispery female voice breathed out a spare, three-note melody that hovered over haunting open chords. The effect was probing and plaintive, like a reminder of an intense, past longing I'd almost forgotten about. Roy looked at me with his usual subdued smile. I smiled back. At this he ejected his CD drive and handed me the CD. The music played on. "You can have it," he said. "I just ripped it."

"Are you sure?" I said, taking it. Inwardly, I was elated. Though he'd offered the CD to me off-hand, I felt his gesture showed he thought me one of his kind, the kind that knew about new music genres and underground indie bands. Roy nodded. He clicked on his laptop like he was going to change songs, but then he didn't, just scrolled. His expression was that of loose concentration, like he was really thinking about the music. He was wearing well-worn jeans and a dark brown T-shirt that said "Life is Golden." Both looked thrown on. I wondered if he'd been out late the night before. I pictured him at some intimate music venue I'd heard of but never been to, wearing this same expression as he listened to an up-and-coming singer-songwriter. I imagined him sticking around after the show, having a serious conversation about the state of the recording industry with the performer, drinking obscure craft beers and getting home around three. Or maybe he got in at dawn, and had just woken up. At this point I realized I hadn't figured Roy's wife into my scenario. I started to picture what she might look like when Roy reached for the stack of proofs and began to leaf through the papers abstractedly.

"I don't know why they send me this stuff," he said. "I can just look at it online."

He said this in an inward, wondering tone, but I instantly felt chastened, like I should have known not to bring them, not to take part in this meaningless bureaucratic task. I looked down at my lap and saw the awkward way I was holding the CD and the broken case, one in each hand. I put the CD between the pieces, then held the case closed with two fingers. I was about to get up when Roy spoke again.

"They really shouldn't be making you do this," he said, this time sounding collusive and empathetic. "Maureen always puts off calling the messenger, then it inconveniences other people."

This mollified me. "It's okay," I said. "I like driving."

"I just don't want you to think you have to like, do everything everyone on the team wants you to do. You can push back, if you want. We've had a lot of turnover, in your position. For a while we just had to make do with temps and then things really fell through the cracks."

"Oh," I said, mortified. "I'm actually a temp. I mean, temp-to-hire."

"Oh really?" he said. "Sorry, I didn't know that." He paused to think for a minute, then smiled. "I hope you'll decide to stay."

I was flattered that he thought it was my choice. "I want to," I said. "Everyone seemed so nice." Then I cringed. I hadn't meant to sound so kiss ass. To mask the cringe I put on a grin. I tried to make it look enthusiastic but could tell from the pull of the skin that it probably looked jumpy and uncomfortable.

He didn't seem to mind though. In fact he seemed a bit self-conscious himself. "Thanks," he said, his voice sincere and small.

On the way home I started wondering if maybe I did actually want this job for real. Obviously, it was a step down, but maybe it would pay okay once I was brought on full time, and this team assistant thing seemed to be what I was capable of right now. I liked that no one expected too much of me. I imagined Roy coming back to the office and how we might become friends, the young, cool duo at the agency with apathetic expressions and exploratory haircuts. I considered asymmetrical bangs.

The next afternoon, I actually asked Maureen for Roy's proofs. I left even earlier, around half-past three, and when Roy opened the door, went in boldly. He got me water, and when he did he poured a glass for himself too. We sipped quietly, indie rock on low on his laptop, the shared gesture of drinking somehow intimate and liquescent. We sat close together, almost touching, chatting about the proofs as he paged through them indifferently, methodically.

Then he said, "This is boring."

I shut up.

"No, I mean," he hesitated. "We don't have to talk about work."

"Okay," I said uncertainly. I wasn't sure if he was asking me to leave. I looked up at him and realized he wasn't. His face was suddenly quite close to mine, though his eyes still had that indolent expression, like he wasn't going to make anything happen but was fine with whatever might.

"Did you like The Supplies?" he said.

It was the CD he'd given me. "I did," I said in as neutral a tone as I could muster up, acting as if I didn't notice he'd closed up the space between us. Of course I was panicked and surprised. I'd badly wanted his approval, maybe even had a bit of a crush on him, but I really hadn't considered that he might really want to start something up with me. I'd actually spent the entire evening before listening to the album, trying to come up with intelligent things to say about it. I'd dug around online to read about the band on Pitchfork, but that had confused me further. The album reviewer seemed more interested in showing off how urbane he was than giving readers a clear sense of the music. He started with a quote from an alt lit writer I hadn't even heard of, then compared The Supplies to a whole bunch of bands I didn't know. After a while I gave up and went on Myspace to listen to the band's older songs, but I couldn't tell these tracks apart from the new ones. I'd gone to sleep with the CD on, hoping to internalize it through osmosis.

"I liked the looping minimalist patterns," I said, rehashing what I'd read in the review. "Sorry, I forgot to bring it."

"No, you can keep it." He pointed at his laptop. "I'm trying to digitize."

"Thanks," I said.

I felt uncomfortable. My long-ingrained, self-conscious self was wrestling with the newer, more nonchalant self I wanted to become. I leaned back against the couch to seem more relaxed. When I did our shoulders touched inquiringly. I twisted slightly toward him. He was looking at me, the edges of his soft breaths reaching out to skim my face. He smiled and I smiled back. Then he leaned in and kissed me.

We kissed for close to half an hour. He moved his face in a calm, practiced way that almost felt like he was teaching me how to kiss. There was a patience to it that I was unaccustomed to, none of the sloppy, drunken overeagerness of the guys I'd hooked up with in college. In moments Roy's hold on me felt deep and involved, but overall it was more sensitive than sensual, somewhat tentative, with an underlayer of friendly apathy. There was no pressure or context. We were like moles, nuzzling against each other in a soft, burrowing way, blind but willing to communicate. Sure, I tried to tell him with my lips. No big deal.

When I left I felt a quiet, focused sort of exhilaration. We'd made out high school style but I felt I'd accomplished something, that I'd grown up, his marriedness somehow adding to my subdued elation, as if I'd gone through some long-awaited rite of passage. It was the beginning of something bigger and longer, I could tell, by the fact that we'd only kissed, like we were capping the end of a good first date. It's a little pathetic to think about now, but at the time my experience with Roy was the most real relationship I'd had in a long time, the kind where you actually met up during the day and talked about work and shared music you liked.

The next morning at the agency I was kindlier toward everyone. Maureen gave me proofs and I went about the aisles floatily. Afterwards Maureen invited me into her cubicle and taught me how to create PDFs from Word documents. I knew how to do this, but I let her show me because she seemed happy to do so. When her phone rang she motioned for me to stay in her cubicle. It was her husband. "He wants to try to leave early today," she said when she hung up, "so it looks like I need to work through lunch."

"Anything I can do to help," I said, and she waved her hand like she wouldn't think of burdening me, but was still grateful that I'd offered. I noticed that she was wearing two different earrings, seemingly on purpose, a star stud in one ear, then a bigger, dangly star in the other. I complimented her.

"Oh, these," she said tugging at her earlobes, embarrassed but pleased.

This seemed to open a small door in her. Until then Maureen's attitude toward me had been that of a kindly governess, treating me like a delicate fawn to be gently guided through a scraggly maze of corporate traps. Now, she seemed to see my potential as a colleague-confidant. She started popping her head over the cubicle wall throughout the day. "One more thing," she'd say, and mention some random office protocol I might find useful later, then share tidbits of her life.

I learned Maureen had joined the firm as a receptionist when her kids were still young, and for eight years, took evening classes at Cal State Northridge until she earned her bachelor's, which got her promoted to her current position. Now, her three sons were all in community college, all still living at home in Oxnard. They were prone to quitting things: Baseball teams, geode collecting, conversations with army recruiters. The animated, worried tone she took talking about her boys made them sound troubled and dangerous, but in reality they seemed simply undermotivated, destined for blue-collar work. I could imagine them spending long afternoons stretched out over their unmade twin beds with PlayStation controllers, playing *Final Fantasy X.*

In the past I might have been contemptuous, but listening to Maureen I felt an indulgent, benevolent warmth. Perhaps her kids would go on to fill small, necessary roles in society, laying bricks and fixing sewage systems, helping people hook up their cable internet.

Driving to Roy's that afternoon I felt a connection to everyone I saw, a deeper sort of understanding about our relatedness that didn't need to be defined in concrete, hierarchical terms. I took time to notice the people inside the cars, their little fidgety preoccupations. Here we all were on our various paths, which weren't so much paths but rather oneiric somnambulations, bumping gently along in the manner of benign bacteria. This is the attitude I should have had all along, I thought, just saying yes to whatever wanted to happen, not in an overt or grabby way, but in a more acquiescent, shrugging manner.

Once I got to Roy's, I tried to adopt that attitude for our make-out session. I felt our need to be close to each other had its own quiet sense of urgency, but when we actually started touching, there was an affectedness to the encounter. He didn't push me, and I wasn't going to push him, so after making out for a while the kissing didn't stop so much as just fade out, until we were just sitting, breathing, and we started to talk in calm, muted tones. In a way this seemed more adult to me, like we were in control of ourselves. It also felt like a passive dare, a weird game of chicken to see who could hold out longer. We talked about music, or rather, he talked, in an offhanded way that made it seem like he assumed I knew what he knew. He used phrases like "fluid atonality"; he compared one singer's voice to Argentinian Malbec. Radiohead was mentioned at times, but only as a basis for comparison for other bands, not as a topic in itself. I nodded along. Roy liked repetitive, cerebral stuff, and for long minutes we just listened to songs, our bodies in slack contact. When the clock said six, he sat up slightly, and I left. I figured his wife came home soon after that, though neither of us ever mentioned her.

At night, in bed in my apartment, I replayed the afternoon in my mind and masturbated. For some reason it took me a long time to come, as if the dawdling way we made out transferred itself to my masturbating. I ran out of memory tape and was forced to start fantasizing. My fantasy had us go to a concert at The Echo. The Echo was all the way in Los Feliz but in my imagined world we took a short walk there holding hands, then stood in line in limpid postures of indifference. Once we got inside we made out in the corner, in much the same manner as we made out at Roy's place, except it was sweatier, from the heat of the crowd. The Supplies played, and live, the band had a more thrumming, insistent beat that urged us on, so that even just kissing, eventually we came—or at least I did, standing pressed against Roy, quietly and secretively and in rhythm.

In the office on Friday though, my imagination was more sedate, realistic. I tried to puzzle out how we would make it work, this affair, once Roy got back into the office. It would probably be easier for him to come to my place after work, I thought, so long as his wife wasn't nosy about how he spent his time. I sketched out a little diagram of my apartment and imagined how I might redecorate to make the place appropriate for the assignations. Right now my place had a dorm-room look. I had to get rid of the plasticky furniture.

I started planning an overhaul, but then got distracted wondering why Roy hadn't tried to sleep with me. When we made out he would run his hands over my body, but only tentatively, without getting probing or forceful. Was he waiting for some sign from me? Or was it because we were technically coworkers? Maybe our well-mannered make-out sessions were his way of drawing boundaries, albeit soft and mushy ones, a way for us to enjoy each other but also avoid repercussions.

Yet I couldn't imagine Roy being this calculating or clinical. His attitude lacked that kind of shrewdness. I imagined him in a courtroom, giving the jury a shrug. Call her my lover if you want, it would say. Plus, the lack of sex was titillating in its own right. I struggled with it but didn't necessarily want to change it. In this way I kept sending myself in thought spirals, and then got annoyed myself for stressing at all. There was something old-fashioned and juvenile about my wanting to figure this out, to define and understand what was happening in fixed terms, I thought. Let it be, I told myself.

———————

That afternoon Maureen gave me the proofs at noon. "We have another blueline," she said. "A one-pager. This one, we have to get to the printer tonight. If you leave now," she looked at her watch, "you should be back in plenty of time."

I felt my face fall. This completely ruined how I thought the evening was going to go with Roy, but of course I couldn't say anything. I took the stack from Maureen without comment. She must have sensed my unhappiness though, because she added, "It's a quickie, so you shouldn't have to wait too long. You're keeping track of the mileage, right?"

"Yeah," I said in a mumble. I shuffled back into my cubicle and morosely picked my car keys out of my purse.

Maureen looked over our shared wall. "Sorry about this," she said. "Really, you've been such a good sport about all the driving. This'll absolutely be the last time. Roy'll be back in on Monday." She paused. "I mean, who takes a whole week off for a simple appendectomy?" She laughed apologetically.

I got to my car in a huff, both angry and anxious. What if this was our last time together? I'd spent a lot of time picturing us tangled loosely on his couch, making quiet but precise plans for future rendezvous, and now there'd be no time for that.

Would we find a way to talk about this stuff at work, after he returned? Or would this rushed last meeting end up making things awkward between us, putting a weird end to all of it?

Once I started driving though, I started to calm down. It dawned on me that I could just make up an excuse to not go back to work. I could call Maureen at five and blame the traffic, or say I got in an accident. Or I could bring Roy into it. He could tell Maureen the proof just took a lot longer than expected, and give her his edits over the phone. I'd heard Maureen do this before, though only with Brian the boss. Debating these options, my mind worked furiously the whole way there, and by the time I got to Roy's place I was filled with a woozy uneasiness. I felt bolder, but scared about it.

Roy too seemed bolder, with a more solid set to his face. His attitude greeting me was different, slightly assertive. This made me nervous enough that going in the door, I tripped and dropped the proofs. They scattered into a loose semicircle around his feet.

He gestured for me to leave them. "Come here," he said. His voice had its usual blasé tone, but when we started kissing I knew it was going to happen this time. We went into his bedroom and sat on his futon-like bed. As we took our shoes off I thought, I'm about to have a real affair, with a married guy. The thought was oddly more tantalizing than the actual feeling of the moment, which Roy still imbued with indolence. I tried to hide my enthusiasm. To appear too willing would be uncool, I thought, taking on Roy's MO.

We lay down. As we started kissing again I grew self-conscious about my body and its newish junk food weight. I tried to wiggle out of my shirt, but it was tight and this didn't work well, so I had to sit up again. When I did I took off my bra too; it had ridden up uncomfortably in the struggle. Inelegantly, I lay back down.

He sent a cautious hand over my breasts, like he was gauging their size, though without judgment. He let his hand trail down under my skirt and slipped it under my underwear. I was surprised at how wet I was. It embarrassed me, because it revealed how badly I wanted this. To counter that I closed my eyes and tried to make as little noise or movement as possible. Still, after just a few minutes I came, the orgasm sharp but also strange because I tried to mask its intensity, the sensation swelling to fill me, but released only in a fearful, hesitant manner, which came out in quick bursts I couldn't control. Afterwards I was left feeling an exhausted sort of tension, both closeted and exposed.

This didn't seem to bother him. He took my underwear off and got on top of me. He entered me first, then we wriggled each other's clothes off, like it was an obligatory step to completing the affair properly. Once we were naked there was a rhythmic, careful quality to the way he moved above me, the same quality he'd had when touching me, and I think it was that detached concentration that turned me on, though I couldn't articulate why, and though through it all I felt powerfully anxious, afraid and excited that I might come again.

It ended just before I did. Afterwards we lay beside each other for a few minutes. He petted my hair distractedly, the intimate way one might a child's while remaining focused on some other task. Then he got up, pulled on his boxers, and brought me a glass of water.

"Thanks," I said.

He smiled, and went back out, maybe for a glass for himself.

I lay back, sipping. I surveyed the room for clues. It was a semi-dark space, the blinds drawn, sparsely furnished like the living room. On the side table there was a small watch, a woman's, face down. Beside it was a digital clock; it read 14:42. There were no pictures around, which I thought was odd. Clearly he liked his life neat and organized. Laying there, I felt good, like a carefully sharpened pencil perfectly fitted into its pencil case. Maybe we'd end up spending more time here. He didn't seem to have any qualms about having sex with me in the bed he shared with his wife. Or maybe this meant he didn't care if she found out, and this whole thing would move faster than I thought. Maybe I'd end up moving in. I tried to picture myself living here, and decided I'd like it, the austere walls, the cool floors. I could get rid of my furniture altogether.

I let my mind wander this way until I realized Roy had been gone for a while. I slid my legs over the side of the bed. I thought about calling him, but it seemed too obtrusive in the zen space. Instead I pulled off the top sheet and wrapped it around me like they do in the movies, then sashayed out, the sheet fanning out behind me like a wedding dress train.

He was sitting on the couch, bent over the blueline.

After a minute, he looked up and saw me. His expression tensed for a second, then returned to its neutral position. "I'm almost done," he said.

I stood quiet for a bit, coming up with a response. "I didn't know you were working out here," I said finally.

"It's due today," he said, turning his eyes to the proof.

Something about the way Roy looked away from me brought up an intense sense of déjà vu. Suddenly I was back in college again, walking into economics class. In the middle of the back row sat a guy I'd hooked up with once, a cute guy I'd been stunned had picked me, he'd had his options at the frat party. Of course we never talked again after that incident, though we saw each other every morning in class. When I entered he'd already be sitting there, blandly watching the door. The first few days our eyes met, and he turned his face away like he was bored, his expression impassive save a hint of a derisive smirk. Each time this happened I felt I'd somehow pestered him and gotten rejected anew. I started bracing myself on my way to class, preparing, deliberately fixing my gaze at a different direction as I walked in. But once in a while I forgot, and I had to see that dismissive, insolent look on his face again.

That was Roy's attitude now, working. Watching him I started getting that *Groundhog Day* feel, like I was watching my life on a loop. I was suddenly overwhelmed by a sense of tired resignation.

Then it occurred to me: there were no classmates watching, no one else for me to be self-conscious about.

I didn't realize this consciously so much as sense it, but sense it I did, because instead of retreating back into the bedroom and leaving demurely, I kept standing there. I started really watching him, hard. And as I bore my eyes into him, I could sense a shift in him too. He was still pretending to mark things, but I could tell by his cultivated concentration that I was frightening him.

"That's right," I said. "Maureen said five at the latest."

I stared at him until finally, he looked up. When he did, he gave me a shaky smile.

"Look, this—We're cool, right?" he said. The voice he used was a firm, I know we can be adults about this tone. But I saw the alarm in his eyes.

I smirked. "Just try to make it quick," I said. I went into the bedroom to get dressed.

When I got back to the office Maureen grinned at me and held out both her hands for the proof like a greedy kid. "Ah, finally," she said. "After this, we're done for the week."

I tried to smile back at her but I knew it didn't look right. I'd decided I wasn't coming back, but didn't have the heart to tell Maureen face to face. She'd been so sweet to me. I had the sense she'd take it personally, especially since I couldn't come up with a good reason to give her for quitting. I turned away and started collecting my things, dropping them into my purse. My hand was on auto-pilot. I threw in a notepad, a post-it stack with some scribbles on it, a staple remover. The last of these I fished back out quickly and replaced on the cubicle desk.

"What's wrong?" Maureen asked.

"Nothing," I said, in that offhand tone I'd been refining. "What do you mean?"

"Did everything go okay at Roy's?"

"Sure." I shrugged unconvincingly.

She paused. "Sorry to make you make that trip, in Friday traffic."

"It's no trouble," I said. But I could hear the tension in my voice, strangled and passive-aggressive. So I kept talking. "It was actually a nice break from the office," I added.

"Well, he'll be back in the office Monday," she said. After that she disappeared behind her cubicle wall and stayed quiet there for the last hour of the work day. Still, when six o'clock rolled around she came around again and said, "So, have a good weekend." At that I got up and gave her a big goodbye hug, which she returned warmly. Afterwards she raised her brows comically and said, "Monday will be here before we know it," as if to break the tension from our moment of connection. We walked to the parking lot together making small talk, then waved to each other driving away.

On my way home I thought about stopping at a 7-Eleven for ice cream, but resisted. I was better than that. Instead, I called Lisa. I'd planned to leave a message but she surprised me by picking up. I told her I wasn't going back Monday.

"Why?" she said. "What's wrong?"

"Nothing," I said. "I'd just like something different."

There was a short silence, then she started in. "You know, it may seem like you have your pick of jobs out there, but it's really not like that. You're putting me in a—It'll be hard to feel comfortable, sending you out on new jobs, if you're just going to suddenly quit like this whenever some little thing isn't to your liking."

I took this in. "Look," I said. "There was this creepy guy, alright? I couldn't take it anymore."

Her tone changed. "Oh, I didn't realize," she said. "That's terrible, terrible. Are you alright?"

"Yeah, I'm fine," I said.

"Sorry about what I said earlier. We take this kind of thing really seriously. You've read our materials . . ." her voice trailed off. "If you want to really address this, we can do that. You're not powerless here. We take the welfare of our employees really seriously."

"No, no," I said. "No, nothing like that." I paused. "I just want to leave before anything like that happens."

"Okay," she said. She sounded puzzled, but mostly relieved. I think she was curious to know more, but not if it was going to create paperwork. When she spoke again, her tone was almost maternal. "We'll find you something else," she said. "I'll call you Monday."

"Something with writing," I said, then added, "if you can."

Once I hung up I wondered if Lisa would say anything to Maureen about this whole alleged sexual harassment thing. I decided nothing would come of it, and that even if it did, no one would suspect Roy. How could they? Looking at him objectively now, I could see him as he was—somewhat effete and asexual-looking, too passive and lackadaisical to force anything on anyone. It was almost strange, what you could see so clearly once you detached from a situation. I was tempted to obsess about why I'd gotten so into him, but I didn't. I had my own life to worry about.

I realized the traffic on Pico was a lot worse than usual. I wondered if there was an accident or construction. Right then, a cyclist went by my window. Then another, and another. I looked up ahead and saw that a couple cyclists were blocking the intersection so the others could get through safely. I looked behind me; there were close to fifty cyclists, weaving jauntily through the lanes.

All the cars were now at a complete standstill. Most of the cyclists moved fairly slowly, careful not to scrape the cars with their handlebars, though a few raced through on their fixies, gleeful and foolhardy. Watching them, the drivers went from angry about the delay to resigned, then curious and friendly. They started lowering their windows; mine was already open because my AC had gone out a few months before.

"Hey, let's trade," said a guy in a convertible to a trio of girls scooting through on beach cruisers. They giggled by. "What are you protesting?" the woman in the Corolla next to me asked animatedly, like she might get out to join. "Nothing," a tattooed guy in spandex told her. "It's Critical Mass."

The woman looked around with alert, manic eyes, like she was anxious for something to happen. Then she pointed. "Hey, I've seen you already," she yelled at a cyclist a lane away. "You just went by."

"It's a Dada-themed ride," he said. "We're going in circles."

"On purpose?" she said, but he was already gone.

It was dusk. We all sat and watched the cyclists like the audience at a drive-in theater. The experience had the stretched-out, dreamy quality of a Godard film, but the whole thing really only lasted only a few minutes; the Dadaists must have decided to move the circle. Traffic started inching forward again. A few straggling cyclists still struggled in the lanes and the cars were genial toward them, slowing to let them wheedle through. Pedaling on, they yelled thank yous and waved, grinning widely like they were the stars of the show.

When the riders turned the corner, the whole block of drivers swiveled their heads to watch them go, though we knew they were headed nowhere, happy and free.

Easy Target

It happened the summer I joined Match.com. I had written a fairly normal profile but at the end tacked on that I wasn't necessarily looking for anything serious, I just wanted someone to make out with. It had been a year and a half since I'd moved back to Los Angeles after college, and I was still that lonely. Predictably, my inbox was always full, mostly with graphic notes pecked out with one hand, which gratified me in a bitter but thrilling way. In comparison, Sam's initial email was sedate, courteous. We both liked Modest Mouse. His profile said he was twenty-nine and six foot three, and showed a decent-looking guy with a conservative haircut, the kind you might see in a Men's Wearhouse ad. He sent me a link to a story in the *Daily Bruin* about UCLA medical students who'd built Habitat for Humanity houses in South LA. He was in the picture, smiling in a construction helmet with his classmates. He said he was going to become an army doctor.

"Does this mean you might go to Iraq?" I wrote.

"It's possible," he wrote back.

"Are you a Republican?"

"Not even!"

We started up a playful correspondence, writing a few times a day. His missives were always smart and somewhat jocular. Then on the fourth day, he sent me another link. "To give you a better sense of who I am," he wrote.

The link took me to a profile on a nudist website. The photo showed a naked man from the back, alone at a beach, running into an ocean that looked turbulent and cold.

I felt annoyed and cheated, but also had the weary sense that I'd more or less expected this, that there was an inevitability to his revelation I'd almost foreseen. And I was curious too, complimented, like maybe he'd appreciated something open and daring in me that I hadn't yet noticed myself. The site was set up almost exactly like Myspace. I squinted at the thumbnails of his "Top 8" nudists, his criteria for the kinds of "new friends" he was looking for, his glowing description of his own body, including proud measurements of his penis. Near the bottom of his profile he had a paragraph warning others about "fakes and posers" who talked a big game online but never materialized in real life.

Until then I'd thought that nudists weren't necessarily sexual thrill seekers, that they were essentially old, fat hippies who liked sunbathing naked. But Sam's profile read exactly as a casual sex want ad. I wrote him as much.

"There are different kinds of nudists," he wrote back.

"Just to be clear, this isn't my kind of thing," I wrote him. "And this website, it seems really time-consuming."

"That's okay," he wrote. "I really was just letting you know something about me. I enjoy our emails."

I couldn't decide whether he was just a normal guy going one step above a Craigslist personals ad, or a sexual deviant. I asked him how he'd gotten into this. I asked about his family, friends, other signs of normalcy. He said his parents were in Florida, and he saw them a couple times a year. He was an only child. As a senior in college, he and a few buddies had gotten into the habit of going to strip clubs regularly, becoming friends with some of the dancers—both the determined ones that danced to pay for college and the ones that did it for coke. Then he wrote, "All of this might be easier to discuss in person."

I agreed apprehensively. We made plans to meet that weekend for drinks at a bar I picked out.

But when I woke up the next day, another email was waiting for me. "Option for Saturday," said the subject. He had forwarded an evite to a party for swingers in their twenties and thirties. It was cocktail party themed, ten dollar cover for men, free for women, at a private home in Eagle Rock. Couples and single women were welcome, but single men were not. Clearly, this was why Sam was trying to rope me in. At the bottom of the evite were a dozen or so guidelines to ensure all activities were consensual, advice of the "ask before you touch" and "it's okay to say no" variety.

Later, in the evening, when I emailed back with my number, Sam called immediately. "I mean, it sounds like we could just hang out and watch," he said. His voice was exactly as I'd imagined from his emails, friendly and amused, laying out his argument with a strategic playfulness, like he was building an elaborate Lego tower. He said he'd never been to the group's events. A friend from his nudist website had just forwarded it to him.

"What if everyone's really ugly?" I said.

"Aren't you curious?" he said.

I had to admit that I was.

———————————

He suggested we still get a drink at the bar first to get to know each other, but I drank a couple glasses of wine as I was getting ready to calm my nerves, and was tipsy when he arrived.

"You look fantastic," he said when I opened the door. I had put on a black silk dress, the backless, slinky kind. "I'll be honest, I was a little worried, but your pictures don't do you justice." I knew he was buttering me up but I told him I was relieved too. He looked clean-cut, with the self-assured affability of a guy picked to play *The Bachelor*. His eyes seemed to be constantly appraising his surroundings, then accepting what he saw equably. Anxious, I hadn't been able to eat much dinner, and when I looked up at him I got lightheaded and giggly. Still, I was glad for the wine. I offered him a glass but he shook his head.

"Not much of a drinker, actually," he said. "Should we skip the bar?"

We drove to the party. I kept up a nervous patter, asking him about growing up in Florida, medical school, the traffic on the way to my place. I was annoying myself with my half-drunk prattle, but he didn't seem to mind it, especially when I started asking about his website again. He talked in a cheerful, instructive tone, like he was explaining a complicated but exciting new scientific finding. I asked him if he'd ever gotten into a threeway. He said he had, once and relatively recently, with a couple he'd met at a bar in Hermosa Beach. I assumed he'd met them through the website but he said the couple had just come up and sat next to him at the bar and started a conversation. The woman was stunning, so when they asked him if he'd be interested, he'd agreed. "She was like, the most beautiful woman I'd ever seen," he said, in a tone of awe that made me feel frumpy. My stomach grumbled.

"With two guys though," I said. "Were you sharing the woman, or did you, like, give him a blow job?"

He paused. "Yeah," he said reluctantly. "That part was weird."

We got there a little after nine. The house was fairly nondescript, a largish family home typical for the neighborhood. The door was ajar. Inside the foyer a short couple stood in front of us, checking in at a table where a woman sat with a list and a red pen. She looked to be in her mid-thirties. Her face was pretty though her eyes had a disappointed droop, the skin around them papery. The couple turned around when Sam and I entered. We all smiled at each other in silence, though I was still pretty buzzed and a part of me wanted to introduce myself, giddily, with hugs.

I peered down the hallway into the living room, but the small portion I could see was empty. Once Sam paid his cover, we walked in behind the other couple. The clatter from my heels echoed through the space. Just as I began to wonder if this party was going to be only the four of us, I saw a couple dozen people standing on the back porch. They seemed to be watching something.

It was a man and a woman having sex, in a room with a glass wall that faced the back porch. Sam and I quietly joined the onlookers, subduing our expressions to adopt the audience's alert yet impassive attitude. The glass took on the qualities of a cinema screen, so watching the couple felt like being in a standing-room-only theater, the crowd facing the stage in mute deference to the actors. Both of them were a bit overweight and plain looking, the kind of people you wouldn't notice on the street. They were in the missionary position. Once in a while the man tried to move the woman's legs up above his shoulders, but the woman was not very flexible, or just preferred her legs where they were. Whenever this happened I had the urge to laugh, because of the wine or the tense air or both, but just grinned stupidly as I watched instead. Mostly the man just thrust on top of her, in a regular rhythm about the speed of a resting heart rate. Her cellulite wobbled to the beat.

"He's her husband," said a woman in front of me rather loudly, talking to a woman to her left while pointing to the woman to her right. "That," the woman continued, pointing to the woman having sex, "is her best friend."

The woman whose husband and best friend we were watching have sex had a beleaguered, so-what smile on her face that made me want to say something nice to her, though I didn't know what. She looked almost exactly like her best friend—both with some extra poundage, both with long, curly hair—except unlike her naked friend she was wearing a cobalt blue dress, with heels dyed to match. I imagined the three of them making the ninety-minute drive into town from Chino, sharing Slim Jims and Fritos and brushing the crumbs onto the car floor.

The couple appeared to have finished. The crowd started shifting uneasily, sizing each other up, unsure how to proceed. Just then a short, studious-looking guy stood up on the couch at one the end of the porch. "Excuse me, everyone," he said. "I'm David, one of the hosts. We're going to play some ice-breaker games over here if you'd like to join us. Otherwise, have fun and enjoy your evening."

Sam said he thought this would be the least awkward way of socializing. I pretended to think this over, though I knew I'd agree—I guess I hadn't ruled him out yet, and in any case, the prospect of striking out on my own made me anxious. "Sure, why not," I said affably. We walked over. As we passed by the couch, David came down from his perch and introduced himself. He complimented me on my dress with a look of enamored appreciation, but in an uneasy tone. I thanked him, my voice chirpy. Next to the couch was an open futon piled with cushions. Sam and I sat down on this, in cozy company with a half dozen other couples. In many ways it looked like a typical cocktail party, the girls all pretty and made-up in their dresses, many of them demure and appropriate for work functions. The guys looked normal, neither more nor less attractive than the average crowd, though better cleaned-up for the occasion. I decided that Sam was the best looking guy there, which made me feel proud, but also disappointed.

The game wasn't so much a game as just a deck of cards players could draw from in turn. Each card had a sexual dare written on it, like "Kiss someone you haven't met yet." "Of course," David said, explaining the rules, "you can always say no. If you don't like the card you get, you can just skip your turn, or give it to someone else who wants it."

The game began. The first to go was David himself. "Kiss the woman or man you find most attractive," he read from his card. "Well, I have to say that would be my wife Laura here. It's her birthday today."

The crowd aaah'd as Laura got up. She was a Latina woman, slim and attractive but with a hardened, rather severe face. "That's so sweet, honey," she said. The couple kissed for a long time, playing it up for the crowd, who clapped and cheered good-naturedly. She was a good four inches taller than David in her heels.

Laura went next. "Let your partner pick a woman or man for you to kiss," she read, then laughed. "Who will it be, honey?" she said. David scanned the crowd like he was thinking. Then he pointed at me.

"Do you want to play?" he asked.

The question took a second to register. Once it did, I sat up in a jolt. "Really?" I said, then "Sure." It was the first thing I could think to say.

I'd kissed girls before, but not since fifth grade. "For practice," we'd said giggling, hands on each other's shoulders. This time, it was for show. Laura came over and took my face in her hands. Her lips were soft, but her mouth had a slightly sour taste, and her tongue felt hard and muscular. As we kissed I thought, I'm kissing a girl at a swingers party. I'm participating. She moved her head a lot, miming passion. When we finished, I heard the crowd cheering, Sam the loudest, his face in a rictus of thrilled enthusiasm. I smiled back at the faces turned toward me until I realized they were waiting for me to pick a card.

"Sam, why don't you go?" I said in what I hoped was a magnanimous tone.

Sam bounded up to get his card. "Give a woman or man a one-minute massage," he read, then looked up, visibly disappointed.

I went to get some water, to get rid of the acrid taste of Laura's mouth. When I came back, Sam was in an enthusiastic threeway kiss with the two chubby women, the wife and the best friend, who were groping his body as they went at it. The best friend was now dressed in a pink number that looked like an eighties prom dress. "Do you and your boyfriend do this a lot?" a shy-looking Indian girl sitting near me asked. "He's not my boyfriend," I said. "We're just friends." She nodded, smiling brightly like this was what she'd been hoping to hear. She introduced me to her boyfriend, a pallid guy with wire-rimmed glasses who looked like a computer engineer. He had a surprisingly firm handshake.

The game seemed to be getting more risqué, but unease gave me an odd tunnel vision; my attention focused on the couple I'd just met. The engineer guy was actually outgoing and funny; he told complicated jokes about French restaurants. As time passed other people lost interest in the game too, until eventually, the game petered out altogether. I realized this when I noticed David was sitting next to me, his elbow brushing against my arm.

"I hope you're having a good time," he said.

I said I was. He said he hoped my boyfriend was too, and I said I'm sure he was, though he wasn't my boyfriend. David seemed to take this as an invitation. He touched my arm, then started stroking it gently with two fingers. He asked if this was okay. I said it was; it seemed rude and prudish not to. David started stroking my arm with his whole hand. His palm felt damp; its clamminess seemed to amplify with each stroke, until it felt like he was trying to transfer the filth of his sweaty hand onto my arm. I started getting nauseous.

"Actually, I need to use the restroom," I said.

The entryway to the foyer was lined with men. I smiled uneasily, speedwalking through. I kept an eye out for Sam but didn't see him. The crowd was getting bolder. An intimidatingly muscular guy stopped me and introduced himself; I shook his hand and asked if he knew where the restroom was. He pointed me to the last door down the hall.

Compared to the rest of the home, which was full of cushions and free-floating blankets, the bathroom was extremely small and spare, without even a mat. I wondered if this was to discourage people from fucking in the room; it seemed to contain the only toilet in the house. On the door was taped a piece of paper printed with a version of the rules I'd seen at the bottom of the evite. Someone had added a twelfth rule at the bottom by hand, in green pen: "Be gentle and communicate! Just because you like it really hard doesn't mean other people do!"

When I went back out I noticed the living room area had been curtained off into smaller sections by strategically hung sheets. The middle space looked like it had been set up for a group orgy, the light muted by the hanging sheets and the floor covered by a big shag rug, heaped with cushions and blankets. No one had taken the bait though. All the sex, if any, seemed to be relegated to the private rooms. Only a half dozen people were in the sheeted space, a few sitting on one of the two couches set against the periphery, a few more standing at the edges of the rug, conversing quietly. On the surface I was at a regular party, with anxious people inspecting each other surreptitiously over their drinks, their expressions of unease tinged with hope.

I sat on the empty couch. I realized Sam was one of the people standing. He was talking to a tiny Japanese girl who didn't speak a lot of English; when he said something, she looked at him blankly before nodding her head and saying "ah, yes." I found this funny. The Japanese girl looked a lot like me, but was smaller, more frail-looking. So Sam had a type. Eventually the girl's boyfriend, a scrawny guy not much taller than her, came to join her, and she put both her arms around him, lacing her fingers and burying her face into his side like a wounded animal. Sam introduced himself to the boyfriend awkwardly, then excused himself. He saw me and walked over, plopped down.

He sighed, then turned to me. "See anyone interesting?" he asked.

"Not particularly," I said. I was sober now, my mood slowly starting to sour. We watched the party continue. Most of the guests were couples who looked like fellow first-timers; they clung to their partners as they wandered around, studying what others were doing without making eye contact. Once in a while a naked person walked through. The exhibitionists generally tended to be on the chubby and hairy side, while the thinner people were more modestly dressed; I wondered if this was a universal tendency. A group of four unhappy-looking girls came in through the gap between the sheets, stood in a row and looked around. I noticed a couple of them notice Sam. Their faces grew alert and animated studying him, but he only glanced at them before returning to staring at the Japanese girl. The four girls looked at each other with surly expressions before queuing back out.

Suddenly I felt very unhappy. I let myself grow disgruntled about the fact that single women were allowed at this party but single men not. I understood why; the place would have been overrun with goggle-eyed, gropey guys otherwise. Still, it seemed unfair that inevitably there were more women than men, giving guys an advantage, as always. I felt Sam had used me; I was a prop he could discard as soon as he got through the door. I was reminded of being back in college, with its 60:40 women to men ratio, the scraggly frat boys that walked around with the attitude of demi-gods in their fleece vests. I remembered some of the parties, the keg beer and dank basements and bathroom hookups. I started going through the faces of the guys I'd slept with, letting the images grow distended and ugly.

A young couple I hadn't seen earlier came in the area. The girl looked like a model, early-twenties, tall and tan with a blond bob. She was wearing long, dangly earrings and a black mini dress that looked bandaged on. Her eyes looked liquid, like she was near tears, or had just yawned. The guy looked a few years older than her, vaguely Persian. He asked if they could share our couch. I slid over toward Sam. The couple sat and started talking softly to each other, looking around from the corners of their eyes.

"Hey," Sam said, his face suddenly close to mine. "Did you still want someone to make out with?"

I felt complimented in a sullen, complicated way, mollified somewhat that he'd assessed his options and picked me, though I didn't like the way he'd made the suggestion like he'd be doing me some sort of favor. Still, I realized I didn't want to wander around the party alone, looking pissed off and rejected like the quartet of girls, while waiting for Sam to finish up somewhere. I thought about my Match.com profile and wanted to live up to it. "Sure," I said. "Why not?"

He was a good kisser. He continuously brushed the hair away from my face. His hands were gentle. He let them drop to my shoulders, then my breasts, brushing over them softly. I opened my eyes and saw that the space we were in was now empty, except for the couple on the other end of the couch. The blond girl was giving her boyfriend a blow job, the slurpy, fervent kind that took a lot of energy.

I closed my eyes again. I let myself enjoy the kissing, sinking into the gentle sensations of pleasure. But eventually I felt myself getting pulled to the floor, which made my dress slide up. Sam's body wedged itself between my legs, his erection poking at me. It felt familiar and somehow inevitable.

After a little while making out like this, he said, "We should really get a condom." This disturbed me; I felt guilty, like I'd asked for it so I couldn't turn into a tease now. I grunted oddly in response. "What?" he said. I said I didn't want to be on the floor. He picked me up and put me on the couch, then said he'd be right back and went off.

The blond girl was still blowing her boyfriend, and when he saw me watching he reached over her and pulled her dress up over her ass, then up to her chest, until she stopped to take the dress off, then returned to the blow job with a theatrical enthusiasm. She was wearing a pink thong. Her small, pink breasts slapped against his thighs.

I smoothed out my dress. Maybe Sam would find someone else. But he returned, naked now, condom in hand, and immediately started kissing me again, aggressively this time. I pushed him away like I was bored. "Look," I said, pointing my chin at the blond girl and her boyfriend. He looked then turned back to me, but I ignored him and focused my eyes on the couple, as if I was deeply engrossed. I can have sex any time, I tried to say with my attitude, but this I don't get to see every day.

Looking back and forth between me and the couple, Sam fidgeted urgently. Eventually his body acquiesced to the situation, and we both just sat watching the couple. This seemed to excite the boyfriend. He leaned forward and tried to push off the thong, which prompted his girlfriend to pull it down and off using her left hand, without pausing the blow job. That accomplished, he put a hand on her head, making it move in long, deep strokes. Then he looked at me. When I met his eyes he reached out his hand and cupped my left breast. "Hey," I said, slapping his hand away. "Don't." Sam piped up too, suddenly protective. "Hey man, she doesn't want that," he said quickly, though in a friendly voice.

The boyfriend took his hand back with a little shrug, as if saying no harm, no foul. Then he gave Sam a little nod, an invitation.

Sam immediately put the condom on. In one quick motion he was on his knees behind the blond girl. He grabbed her hips, aiming, then pushed inside her.

At this the girl's body lurched forward and she raised her head slightly, her face in shock. For a second I thought something big might happen.

But then her expression changed, and when her boyfriend pressed down on her head she bent down to the blow job again, though it was harder for her now, her body rocking with Sam's thrusts. Her face turned red, damp with sweat and slobber. Her dangly earrings spasmed, shock-waving in tempo. I felt bad for her. She was a really beautiful girl, someone who could have her pick. I wondered why she was with this guy. Self-esteem issues, maybe, or money. His watch looked expensive.

Finally her boyfriend came, partly in her mouth, partly on her face. At this the girl put her head down on her boyfriend's thigh, twisted away, while Sam pounded on. I noticed the boyfriend and Sam avoided looking at each other, keeping their eyes focused on the blond girl's body. Then Sam thrust really hard. The girl's body suddenly jerked, then stiffened in pain. "Wait," she said, then more uncertainly, "That hurts."

"What?" Sam said.

"I want to stop," she said.

"Do you want to go into another room?" Her boyfriend tried a concerned tone.

"No, I want to stop."

"Okay," Sam said. He was still inside her. "Is it okay if we just go a little longer so I can come?"

The girl hesitated, then said okay, though Sam was looking at the boyfriend when he'd asked the question. As soon as Sam started moving again, I could tell the girl was in real pain, her body rigid, braced against him. He was going really hard. There was a part of me that felt responsible, felt like I should say something, but then again she'd given her consent. I thought about leaving but that felt wrong too, like I'd be abandoning her. And watching her, even wincing with her, I realized a part of me felt relieved, like I'd dodged a bullet. I told myself it would end soon but Sam kept drawing it out, speeding up then slowing down. The girl dug in her elbows and buried her face in the couch, between her boyfriend's legs. Her boyfriend put her hand over his penis, trying to get her to play with it, but she just let her wrist dangle loose and he let it be. People started coming in the space, but she seemed too in pain to notice or care. A girl in a blue dress sat down next to me. Sam introduced himself to her, grinding ostentatiously. "You like to watch?" he said. "Oh, yeah," she said.

As soon as Sam came he pulled out and got up. He looked around at the half-filled room like he was preening, then pulled off the condom and went to throw it away. When he left I looked at the girl. She was sitting on the floor alone with her legs tucked under her, her head downturned, trying to get her dress right side out. Her boyfriend handed her the thong, then looked up at me, proudly, like he'd just taken his bows.

I went to the bathroom again. I felt nauseous. I tried sticking my fingers down my throat, but couldn't get myself to throw up, then I realized someone was knocking at the door. When I opened it I saw it was the blond girl, dressed again. I was about to say something, I felt I needed to acknowledge what had happened somehow, but she just brushed past me and closed the door. She hadn't recognized me.

———————————

We left soon afterwards, but it was a little past two in the morning when we got back in the car. On the drive back Sam was hyped up and garrulous, like I had been on the drive there. He talked in an excited patter.

"That guy David," he said. "When we were leaving, he was like, 'see you next week.' It's going to be a flapper theme."

"Wow," I said. "Well, I definitely won't be there."

He paused. "You didn't have fun?"

I was going to say something else, but checked my response. Instead I said, "I think I would start to lose my grip on reality, if I went regularly."

"You're right," he said quickly, eager to be agreeable. "So what was your favorite part? Of the night, I mean?"

"Huh?" I said. He was irritating me. "What was yours?"

"When we were on the couch, with that other couple," he said. He turned and looked at me like he'd paid me a compliment. "What did you think of them? They were good-looking, right?"

"Sure," I said, and shrugged. "Why not."

When he dropped me off, I felt too exhausted to shower, though I'd wanted to. I just took off my dress and shoes and dropped into bed. But then I couldn't fall asleep. I tried masturbating, to help bring the night to some kind of closure, but I was too tired to come. I thought about the damp trail David left on my arm with his clammy hand, the four roving girls with their looks of dejection, the blond girl's blank, glassy eyes.

Something about those eyes reminded me of the Match.com pop-up I'd clicked on the day I joined. It was one of those collage ads, a dozen or so headshots organized in a grid with the text "View Singles in Los Angeles" at the bottom. The pictures looked just casual enough to pass as ones regular people might put up, but at least in my memory, the faces still all had that symmetrical, bland look of stock photo models. I wondered why those plastic heads had made me click and go on to create a profile. Maybe it was exactly that look that triggered a coercive, egotistical arousal in all of us, benign attractiveness somehow announcing itself as an easy target to play out self-seeking behavior. Because despite the glassiness, the blond girl did have a lonely mournfulness to her, the kind that made her seem like the type who'd closet herself to suffer in silence.

I wondered if I had the same look. Then I remembered my own profile, that line about wanting to make out. I remembered some of the messages I'd received: "I have measurements and pics. You won't be disappointed." Or more directly, "Make out means oral?" I was aggravated at myself for thinking Sam's message was any different. The image of the blond girl's body jerking in pain flashed in my mind again. I let my mood sink and wallow in a morass of disgust and defensiveness and pity and self-blame. I tried to shape for myself a hard definition of trauma and abuse, then thought, well, maybe she was asking for it, which made me snigger out loud. I stopped and sighed. I knew I was just laughing at myself, but it felt good anyway, to be able to make fun of someone, or something.

The Robertson Case

In line to pay for a turkey sandwich at my neighborhood grocery store, I heard one cashier say to another, "That should teach you the perils of pride." She said it laughing, like it was a joke, but the other girl twisted her mouth and said, "Yeah, the perils of telling you." Then she swiped my sandwich over the scanner and looked up at me, hard, like she expected me to speak up and show I was on her side. "I don't need a bag," I said.

Those were the types of exchanges I'd been having lately. The kind that didn't involve me, but with lots of meaningful eye contact.

When I got back home, a girl I hadn't talked to since college had emailed out of the blue. She asked, "Did you hear about Allen?" He had been crushed in a freak accident involving a crane, spent a week in a coma before they pulled the plug. Reading this, I was surprised to find myself growing darkly gleeful, surprised that my feelings about him were still strong enough to elicit this response, four years after graduation. Allen was the first guy I'd slept with in college, though I knew he had a girlfriend who went to another school. He was shy in bed but gave great full-body massages. We'd have quiet sex in his dorm room then lie awake in the cold dark, him talking about his conflicted feelings about me and his girlfriend in excited, breathless tones that were oddly infectious. Of course the affair was brief, but I'd trusted him and it ended badly, spectacularly, so that the rest of my time there I imagined everyone on campus looked at me with an aloof distaste and pity. In those years I nursed revenge fantasies about hurting him somehow, exposing him as some kind of fraud, one-upping him in some life competition. Those more or less ended when I moved back to Los Angeles, leaving behind the Pennsylvania college town and its petty, ruminative drudgeries.

"It's scary," my college friend wrote. "People our age are already dying."

"So great to hear from you!" I wrote back. "How goes it in the Windy City?"

I closed my laptop and looked out the window. It was just beginning to get dark. I started dressing. My friend Erin and I were going to a cocktail mixer for professional singles in their twenties and thirties. Erin had found out about the event through a coworker in the know; to get on the list for the mixers, you had to be invited by someone already on the list. It was at Evoq, a posh newish bar in Hollywood I hadn't been to. I put on a black scoop-neck tank, a tight, black pencil skirt that hit just above the knee, fishnet stockings, and red heels with pointy toes.

Erin picked me up. "Fishnets?" she said. "It's supposed to be like an after-work event."

"I could wear this to work."

"The skirt, maybe." She gave my outfit another once-over. "Who wears fishnets to work?"

"The ones planning to go to mixers afterwards," I said. "Like people are really going to show up wearing their work clothes at this thing. Watch—we're going to be the underdressed ones there."

Erin checked the rearview mirror a little gloomily. She had on a pinkish beige skirt suit, the pressed jacket perfectly fitted over her thin shoulders. Her blouse was a rich cream. She looked liked a kept woman, somewhat demure, almost docile. She was wearing pantyhose.

"You look great," I said. "Expensive." I waited until she smiled thinly. "This guy I dated in college would always freak out when I wore fishnets, said I'd die of frostbite. This was in the winter. He liked them though. He'd take them off then rub my legs warm. I heard he died recently, but not of frostbite."

Erin crinkled her eyes, then cocked her head at me, snorted. "Dated? Or slept with?" she said.

At the mixer we headed straight to the bar, then stayed there—a good vantage point. We'd arrived on the early side; the place was just starting to fill up. Two guys that looked about our age in tailored suits came next to us in the bar to order their drinks. One was cute, with a chiseled jawline and sandy blond hair that looked professionally tousled. He seemed snobbish, held his face tilted up so he was literally looking down his nose. The other looked Jewish and nervous, driven—good on paper. He caught me studying them and smiled, introduced himself and his friend. The guys were both lawyers, first-year associates at the same firm. The nervous one, Jonah, said he went to Harvard for both undergrad and law.

"My sister went to Harvard," I said.

"What house?"

"House? I don't know."

"Those shoes are fierce," he said. "Do you work in the industry?"

I heard Erin snort again, then shrink into herself a little, embarrassed at the loud noise she'd made. The cute guy turned to look at her with a mild disgust, then politely rearranged his face. "I'm a writer," I said. "At this trade magazine company."

Jonah and I split away from our friends. We talked about restaurants and yoga. When I told him I majored in English, he went through what he read in college: lots of Nietzsche, some Edith Wharton. "I'd never have known pickles and donuts had to do with sex," he said about *Ethan Frome*, then giggled. I laughed with him and he said, "It's so great to meet someone smart here." He squeezed my arm gamely with a sweaty hand. "Can I get you another drink?" The crowd at the bar was now three deep but he elbowed his way through, came back almost instantly holding two pinktinis, grapefruit-vodka cocktails that were the night's seven dollar special. I was impressed by his uneasy determination. "Let's sit down somewhere," he said, and led the way to an empty booth in the back.

The booth was like a cave, darkly set apart from the rest of the bar. Even the music sounded muffled. "It's quiet here," I said. "Nice."

He was a gulper, draining his drink as soon as we sat, like he was completing a prerequisite task. He said he and his friend, Brian, had gone straight from work to happy hour to here. "I actually don't drink much usually," he said, "if you can tell." He looked at me with glassy eyes. I shook my head. He started talking about his law firm, began a story about a partner he didn't like, then fluttered his hands like he was erasing the air. "Ugh, I don't want to be one of those guys who always talks about work," he said. His gestures turned more languid, as if his hands were moving through a viscous gel. I watched them like I would a lava lamp. "There's this restaurant I want to take you to," he said, slurring a little.

Suddenly he took both my hands in his and pulled me toward him. His kiss was overlong and slightly suffocating, with a beseeching quality that I found slightly endearing. Afterwards he shifted closer. We spent the night that way, pressing together inelegantly, then exchanged numbers when the event ended.

The drive back, Erin looked defeated. She said she'd wandered around for a while but no one paid attention because all the other girls were in tiny cocktail dresses. So she'd gone back to her spot at the bar. Jonah's friend was still there, and they had a forced conversation just to occupy themselves.

"He asked me what I did for fun and I said I went to museums and galleries," she said.

"Since when?"

"I know. Then I said, 'No I don't. I don't know why I said that.' Then I went to the bathroom."

For our first date Jonah took me to Hump, a high-priced sushi spot at Santa Monica Airport I'd never been to. It was a busy night and we got the last table, a round one that seated five in the middle of the restaurant, brightly lit like we were on stage.

He made a show of picking a sake from the list. He said he'd lived in Japan for six months, working, between undergrad and law school. The waiter brought big white plates, each with eight long pale strips of translucent sashimi, arranged like starbursts and topped with delicate garnishes—thin slices of jalapeño, slivers of jicama. Jonah gave me a slightly disapproving look when I mixed the wasabi with the soy sauce. "They don't do that in Japan," he said, then smiled forcibly to soften things.

I shrugged. "So what do they do in Japan?"

I watched his mouth move in time with his voice. He spoke quickly like he was afraid of losing my attention, punctuating his remarks with chuckles, his hand over his mouth when it was full. He seemed eager to please, which flattered me. In the short silence between sentences, a look of apprehension would creep over his face. Then he'd gulp more sake and start talking again. He said he moved here after law school just six months ago. Work could be brutal, he said. He hinted that he made a lot of money, but made clear he didn't think it was enough. From what he described of his lifestyle he seemed wealthier than any guy I'd dated. This made me feel powerful in a passive kind of way.

Soon the sake loosened his face to a giddy droop. He ordered more. As a non sequitur he told me his grandmother would like me. I said I wasn't close to my family, but that it didn't worry me, I enjoyed the freedom. He looked at me quizzically. He asked me if I thought family was important. "I'm not sure what that means," I said. "It's not something I think about too much at this point in my life. I'm more focused on my friends, and meeting new people." He nodded fervently.

The new sake arrived and he poured more, ordered dessert.

With the next drink what remained of his nervousness seemed to slink away. His posture sagged, though he retained his impatient quality. He gripped my arm and pulled me toward him, but he hadn't measured the distance right and he almost pulled me off my chair. "Careful," I said. "These seats are wobbly."

I saw his mouth open wide as it neared my face. He was clumsy but insistent; once we started kissing it was hard to pull away. He had mentioned a girlfriend the first year of law school and I wondered if that was the last time he'd had sex. The waiter set down the green tea ice cream with a smirk.

Finally I whispered, "The dessert's here."

He stopped chewing my ear, quickly picked up a spoon. "They make their ice cream in-house," he said in a tone of embarrassed cheer. He tried to pour me more sake but he'd already drained the bottle. He asked for the check and paid it.

As we walked back to the car his anxiety returned full force. He was holding my hand but looked lost in thought, his expression almost angry. When he caught me looking at him, he unknitted his forehead and smiled unconvincingly. "That was fun," he said.

In the car we fogged up the windows. The desperate quality of his need made me reticent, much more reserved than usual. I didn't know what to do with my hands. I kept putting them on his chest, pushing him away slightly. I didn't want clothes coming off in the parking lot; I remembered how Erin had said "Dated? Or slept with?" in that resentful tone of hers. I could tell Jonah was trying not to appear too pushy but having a hard time of it. My mouth felt raw; he had this aggressive way of sucking my lip. Finally he pulled away, fell back into the driver's seat, breathing hard. He looked at me with a mix of desire and dissatisfaction, then suddenly grabbed my hand and rubbed it against his crotch, hard, three times. He let go, waiting to see what I would do. When I moved my hand away his face contorted into a frustrated cringe. Then he recovered. He smiled, teeth gritted with a mock confidence, like this was about how far he'd expected things to go, and he respected me for it. I smiled back.

About a week later, it was my birthday. Jonah called with brief, happy wishes, made plans to take me out that weekend. I imagined what Erin's voice would sound like when I told her about it, but instead of her usual call she sent me an ironic e-card. "Let's celebrate the first time you cried naked in someone else's bed," it said. In the message section she wrote, "Champagne brunch with the girls at Lago Sunday?"

On Friday Jonah showed up with a book—a big, hardback Yoga basics book that I'd seen on the $4.99 sale table at Barnes & Noble. He handed it to me in a wrinkled gift bag that looked reused. "Thanks," I said. "I thought about getting this book." It had been a long while since a guy had gotten me a gift.

We went to Monsieur Marcel, an open-air restaurant on a pedestrian shopping street in Santa Monica. We had trouble keeping up a conversation but pretended we were enjoying a comfortable silence. He ordered generously. He was an odd contradiction—cheap gifts, expensive meals. He drank less this time, stayed tense, but he worked hard to affect a laid-back attitude. The result was unpersuasive, but his effort warmed me to him. Waiting for the check, he slipped his hand under the table like a tentacle. My hand was on my lap and he gripped both my hand and the thigh beneath it, squeezing. "You're good company," he said. He smiled with an anxious flinch.

"You too," I said. I put my other hand above his hand. "You have nice hands," I said.

I'd already planned on sleeping with him that night, but he worked hard to talk me into going to his place, said his wine club had just sent some bottles and we could watch TiVo. Once we got in the car he turned less handsy and more officious, like he was biding his time before the big attack. He lived in a high-rise in Westwood, the kind with a valet. As we took the elevator up to the ninth floor I thought I felt a mix of excitement and dread, like I was about to take a big test I'd overprepared for.

"Study harder!" I said, when he opened the door. I was reading aloud his laptop screensaver's scrolling green text.

He cringed. "I haven't changed it since law school," he said.

He showed me a bottle of Sangiovese, holding it at an angle like a sommelier, then looked up to see my expression. I raised my eyebrows and murmured something vaguely complimentary. He poured the wine into tall glasses without rinsing out the dust.

We started watching an episode of *24*. I'd never seen the show before and couldn't follow the plot. Kiefer Sutherland was sweating while driving an SUV. "He developed an addiction while undercover," Jonah said, then put his arm around my shoulders like this revelation brought us closer.

"So he's the good guy," I said.

"More or less," he said, then, "Yes."

I slipped my shoes off and pulled up my knees, leaned my legs over his lap. His apartment took on a stage-like quality, where none of the actions seemed real. At the first commercial, he turned his head and covered my mouth in his suffocating way.

For a while I tried mirroring his enthusiasm, hands and mouth moving in grabby circles that seemed apologetic, then angry and demanding. Occasionally I could feel my desire shift inside me, but only in an abstract, underwater way.

He suddenly pulled back. "I have to go in to work tomorrow."

"That's okay," I said.

His lips curled up in a quiet, satisfied manner. He quickly restraightened them, then smiled with teeth. I smiled back. He pulled me into him. I turned my head so his mouth moved onto my cheek, my neck. His lips felt soggy and glutinous.

He pulled me down to the floor, into the space between the couch and the coffee table. It was a really narrow space, with the glass edge of the coffee table partially above us. It reminded me of being on Allen's top bunk bed, so close to the ceiling we'd had to move cautiously. With Allen's body over mine I'd had the sensation of being boxed in and pinned down, vulnerable under his cool, shy hands. Allen was always timid to start, but unstoppable after that. The first time we slept together he kept thrusting after he came, so the condom rolled off and lodged inside me in a coil. He was gentle as he reached his fingers in to drag it out, apologizing. Maybe he liked that moment of tenderness. Maybe that's what I liked too, the collusion, cleaning up the small, organized mess of planned mistakes.

Jonah's ad-hoc floor space was even tighter. With much effort he managed to unbutton my shirt and take it off, first lifting one shoulder and twisting out an arm, then the other. I could barely move, only shift a little. At first my inertness seemed to make him self-conscious, but then he took to it, asserting his will without preamble or apology. He bit my breasts, gently at first, and then with aggression. He clawed down my stomach, then started fiddling with the clasp to my pants. He had trouble with it but didn't seem to want help, wanted to show me he could figure it out. He wriggled uncomfortably, rubbing his erection against me. He tried pulling at my pants again, and this time, hit his funny bone on the coffee table with a loud bang.

"Are you okay?" I said.

"That hurt." His voice was small and angry.

"Do you want to stop?"

"If you want to." He seemed to be seething, even bared his teeth. Then he turned up the corners of his mouth to mimic a sad smile.

I sat up. "Well," I said. "Since you're working tomorrow."

He watched me button my shirt.

"I guess I should get home," I said.

He flinched, then his manners came back. "It's still early," he said, "if you want to hang out for a bit."

I got up, then plopped down heavily on the couch. My limbs felt heavy and lax, like they preferred their previous catatonic state. "Okay," I said. I stifled a yawn. "I've been really lethargic lately for some reason. It isn't you." I let my head fall back so I was looking up at the ceiling. "Actually I found out someone I knew from college died. Someone I dated. It wasn't serious but it was intense, for a little bit. Physically intense. I mean, it was someone I used to sleep with."

He was quiet and I couldn't see his expression. I heard him lift himself up to the couch. There was a long pause.

"Do you want to talk about it?" he said.

"No," I said. "Not at all. I don't know why I brought it up. I barely knew him and it wasn't a big deal. But thanks."

24 was still playing. We watched without interest. Jonah started rubbing my neck and shoulders, awkwardly, his arm crooked in a weird angle against the back of the couch. I turned to make it easier, and he pulled me against him so my back was against his chest, our heads turned to the right to face the screen. He eased his hands down to my stomach, then swirled them around in small, massaging circles. The circles slowly grew bigger, until his hands were grazing the bottom part of my breasts, then eventually brushing over my nipples, surreptitiously, like he was hoping I wouldn't notice and stop him.

Finally I said, "Should we go to your bedroom?"

"If you want to," he said quickly.

His bed looked like it had just been made. I eased my shoes off and lay down. I realized I was tired; I felt my body fall for what seemed like miles. I closed my eyes. In a minute he started to touch me, but I stayed still, which felt interesting, almost pleasurable. When I opened my eyes again he gave me a look of confusion and veiled repugnance. At that I mustered up my strength and sat up, took my clothes off like a Band-Aid before sinking back again. I watched him undress hurriedly, trying to shield his middle; he wasn't overweight, but a little soft. He covered my body with his. He rolled around on top of me grabbing and sucking parts of my body, at times self-consciously, at times more heatedly. I veered between feeling guilty for not being more involved, and feeling entertained with a sort of cruel mirth. Occasionally, I wanted to laugh out loud. He seemed to be really exerting himself, working hard for a reaction.

He touched me between my legs. "Should I get a condom," he said. His face had a somewhat grim, expectant look.

"Okay," I said.

He sat turned away from me to put on the condom, then hurriedly flipped on top of me, hiding himself. He fucked me in a furtive, discomfited sort of way, not meeting my eyes—quick, strained thrusts, then a suppressed grunt when he came. It was over quickly.

Afterwards, he immediately snapped up and near-ran to the bathroom to throw the condom in the trash. When he came back, he had on boxers and a look of self-loathing.

"Hey," I said.

We settled into bed, but I could tell he wanted me to leave. I stayed naked, my head on the pillow with the comforter up to my waist, and that seemed to make him uncomfortable. He offered me a T-shirt but I declined because I didn't want to bother sitting up to put it on. He sat upright a foot away from me, and when he talked he stared hard at my face, his eyes tense and fixed away from my breasts. After a few minutes he said he needed to check his email for work, and I said "mm-hmm" and blinked softly, like I was falling asleep. He turned out the light and left the room.

I too wished I was in my own bed, but the effort to dress myself and drive home felt too great. I wondered why we'd forcibly put ourselves through the trouble of sleeping with each other, like we were both trying to prove something about ourselves. I tried to remember why I'd slept with Allen, but the feelings I could recall were too filled with the angst of the relationship's ending. I couldn't remember any of the exact words Allen had said, just the tones of his voice—warm and shy and bewildered at the beginning, hard and unforgiving at the end. What I recalled more clearly were the fantasies I indulged in after it all ended—both the sweet drama of painful reconciliation and the violent red crush of his head under my heel.

I stretched out in shavasana pose and breathed deeply to induce sleep. Through the door I heard Jonah's voice on the phone. He said something that sounded like "obdurate fish." I thought he was insulting me, but I must have misheard, because then I heard him say, "It's part of the Robertson case." He sounded cold and cynical, like a man in the know.

The Locust of Desire

boy with black arm socks at Insomnia—Los Angeles
You're not the usual guy I date, but maybe it's practical to date men your friends find slightly repulsive.

blue polo shirt guy at Urth Caffé—West Hollywood
You were with a girl who I think was your girlfriend, but you looked unhappy. I overheard you say something about the locus (locust?) of desire. The most important moments are the most mundane ones enacted at the right places, then narrated with insolence.

caffeinated dogwalker at Coral Tree Café—Brentwood
We were there before the lunch rush. You gently tied the leash to the parking meter, gave each dog an approval pat before going in. The intimate relationship between strangers.

gray suit sans tie at Bread & Porridge—Santa Monica
You looked a little breathless, like you'd been running, standing by the eye-level shelf with its eight glasses, lined up, lip down.

Above, a bronze ceiling fan spun athletically. Cheap brown leather couches crowded into a blank space punctuated by a few large, leafy floor plants. They matched each other, but nothing else. In the corner, a stand of condiments and five wooden pepper mills watched us inhale, exhale in harmony. You were the perfect complement to the setting.

boy eating herring at Warszawa—Santa Monica
You watched my surreptitious shedding of socks, laughed back when I looked up and noticed you were watching. Later, your friend came over and asked to buy me a drink. Societal norms seem an overwrought mass of laughable formalities, don't they?

boy in oversized art books section at library—Downtown
By the time you walked in, everyone else already looked like they'd come to terms with their loneliness.

guy with green bookbag in Fairmont Hotel—Santa Monica
You were walking with someone who looked like your father, and I think you thought I was looking at him. I'd like to think of myself as the kind of girl who has affairs with older men, that I give them a fair shot to turn me on. But it's impossible to get past the receding hairline, the slightly protruding belly, the striped golf shirt, the sunburned and overeager smile. I was in the narrow bar with my laptop open, playing business girl getting a few clicks of work done before the big industry conference tomorrow. Maybe you're too young to join me for a drink, but I hope you'll relish the anonymity of the city. Strangers, whether

desirable or frightening, will disappear forever by the eleven a.m. checkout time.

guy with black hat at Stephen Cohen—Los Angeles

When we spoke, I had a hangover pain under my left eye. Everyone else had been to therapists with the same training as mine. When I opened my mouth, they looked at me actively and punctuated the ends of my sentences with an individualized assent that sounded unlike the usual uh-huh. Today, the physical pain isn't as acute. The people we know are completely random. And I suppose there's a beauty in it, but most of the time it just seems like a fucking mess.

boy reading *Monkeybicycle* at Dutton's—Brentwood

I could see you were reading a poem, tracing your finger below each line to focus an attention that wanted out. I remember liking the idea of poetry, but now it's difficult for me to figure out what, if anything, I enjoy. Meaning: everything seems enjoyable in a stuffing-envelopes sort of way. Stuffing a lot of envelopes and watching a stack grow becomes mildly satisfying. Write and black letters fill up a page, except there's that question of substance. I suppose you could get nitpicky about stuffing envelopes too—folding letters in perfectly creased thirds, moistening the lip of the envelope without wobbles, putting the stamp on an exact eighth of an inch in from both the top and right edges. With poetry I can be attentive—pay attention to handwriting, grammar, syntax, all of that—but in the end I may as well have filled the pages with *s*'s. Or *o*'s. Or just diagonal slashes.

The Regulars

The morning of Erin's birthday, I called it quits with Blake. The break was all in my head; I didn't try to talk to him because I thought he might act like I was wasting his time, calling him about something so trivial. Still, I found myself seething in the slack pockets of the day, turning over in my mind one or another deprecating thing he'd said. He'd been intense in bed but sadistic outside it, criticizing what I wore, how I ate, though I wasn't overweight, just not lean like he was. He was rarely free. I'd meet him at his place after work, and he'd fuck me in his bathroom where he was getting ready to go out again, usually to some nebulous work function, though I'd stopped asking. Afterwards he'd grab a handful of my ass and say he liked having something to hold on to, in a tone that suggested he didn't. Then he'd squeeze and laugh.

Mostly, I was angry at myself. I had allowed his casual cruelty. I had let him redirect his self-loathing out at me. That said, my memory of him, of all my relationships, had a remote, otherworldly quality I could almost dismiss as a dream.

That night Erin decided we'd go karaokeing at Backstage. "There's nowhere to sit," she yelled when we got there. She didn't sound particularly peeved by it though. We'd taken a cab, already drunk from our happy hour turned late dinner. Erin scanned the crowd purposefully, her eyelids in a droopy leer. A girl in a tight black tank and muffin top jeans was singing "The Locomotion." Her friends gyrated frenetically in front of the stage, beers in hand. I spotted a quartet of college guys spread out over two tables on the wall facing the stage. I asked if we could squeeze in, using big, exaggerated gestures to communicate over the music. They scooted over. The boy at the end said something unintelligible as I sat next to him. I scanned the crowd at the bar.

"You don't remember me," I heard the guy speak again, louder this time, at the back of my head. "When you came over I thought maybe you did."

I turned. "We've met?" He was smiling. He was on the pale side and had the face of a bashful teenager. He wore black, boxy glasses which helped make him look slightly older, in a vaguely corporate way.

"I work at Intelligentsia," he said. "I made you a latte. Last week."

I remembered the latte. I'd ordered it after waiting twenty minutes for Blake to show, which he did right after the barista told me I had a great smile, and that the drink was on the house. I'd been too focused on Blake to say thanks. "Do you always wear glasses?" I asked.

He smiled; he hadn't heard me over the music. He asked me if he could buy me a drink.

I took a minute to answer, and in the pause he blurted, "I'm twenty-two." He looked embarrassed, though he held my gaze. I shrugged and told him I was twenty-nine. He nodded like he'd already known this but was glad to hear me say it anyway.

At this, I suddenly found myself drawn to him. He seemed open and untouched, like someone I could have a pure exchange with.

His name was Matt. He'd majored in business at USC, then taken a year off to travel around Europe and Asia. Now he was killing time working at the coffee shop for a few months before starting his job at a mobile tech company where he'd interned one summer. He acted impressed that I was a freelance writer. He said he'd never been good at writing. I told him I didn't write anything original, just followed a format and formula, but he looked at me like he thought I was being modest. As he finished his drink my Mai Tai arrived; I hadn't had one since college but I'd wanted something sweet. We shared it, then he ordered another. We put in some songs but they didn't come up. He said he enjoyed traveling but that a year may have been too long, that he was ready to "start real life." I told him I was too, although I didn't really know what that meant anymore. He nodded seriously.

"You must give out a lot of free lattes," I said.

I assumed he'd deny it, but when he kept smiling shyly and said, "No, I really don't," I believed him.

By this time we were both pretty drunk. Two overweight guys sang "Last Dance with Mary Jane" as an off-tune duet, hands on each other's shoulders. The bar started to empty. When Matt's friends left, I looked around for Erin and finally saw her in partial shadow at the left corner of the stage, making out heavily with a dark-haired guy. He was grabbing at the backs of her thighs. His T-shirt had rolled up a little, revealing a hint of a beer gut. They were really grinding into each other, her breasts mashed against his chest. Watching them, I became very aware of Matt's body, or how aware he was of his. His movements seemed to get smaller, like he was afraid if he touched me, I'd disappear. This made me feel more receptive and encouraging. The cocktail waitress came over and Matt cut his hand across his throat.

Outside the moon looked liquid, like it had melted a little. The sky was inky, glimmery. When I turned my head the moon too seemed to move, leaving a streak as in a long exposure photograph. Matt's eyes looked glassy, his face delicate and malleable. I watched the moon on his glasses, thinking about the eager way he shared my drink, the fragile reserve in the way he gestured. His open manner was sweet, but it was the reticence that made me see him tenderly. I didn't think I could ease it, exactly, but I wanted to touch it, feel its texture on my skin.

He was parked three blocks away on a residential street. When we got there I kissed him, just our lips touching, his hand on the passenger door he'd been about to open for me. Afterwards we stood in the cold looking at each other.

"I should get home," I said.

He drove. Time warped to slow motion, blurring the lights in Culver City, then skipped forward in staccato rhythm. Some moments, I got mesmerized by the trees whipping by, then gradually came back into awareness.

"That guy you were with last week," Matt said.

"That's over."

"Oh." He paused. "I wasn't sure. I thought maybe he was your boss or something."

I felt my anger rise again. The coffee date had been one of the rare times Blake had agreed to meet me outside his apartment. But he'd sat facing the door, watching the steady parade of women in yoga halters and skinny jeans. He didn't touch me except when he accidentally kicked me under the table, twice. He didn't order anything, just scowled every time I sipped my latte. Finally he asked me if I could drink any slower.

"No, not my boss," I said. "Nothing that intimate."

Matt laughed. He put his hand over mine and stroked it gently. I turned my hand over to hold his. It was warm, rougher than I'd expected. I started idly playing with his fingers. When I looked over at him his face was in deep concentration, driving with one hand.

We climbed the stairs to my studio. I didn't bother turning on the light but the moonlight streamed in the balcony windows so we could see, if only dimly. For a minute we stood awkwardly by the couch, looking at each other. "It must be nice, living by yourself," he said.

Once he started kissing me, he was more confident. He moved me toward my bed, took my clothes off, and pushed me on my back. Then he undressed, unhurriedly, watching me. When he went down on me I came hard and fast, like I'd been suddenly thrown open. Then I went down on him. Afterwards we dozed off, then woke and had sex at dawn. His body moved with an unexpected assertiveness. He asked me to bite his ear. "What else do you like?" I asked. "Just this," he said, pulling me closer to him.

When I woke again the sun had lit up the apartment, bleaching the sheets a blizzard white. Matt was still asleep. His body was splayed out, limbs loose. There was a careless trust in his posture that I immediately wanted to prod at, complicate. I sat studying him. Once in a while his hands would stretch open then curl back around into a loose, ineffectual grip, like a baby's. Noticing this, I grew embarrassed. I remembered his nervous face when he told me he was twenty-two. But I also felt he'd gently nudged open a small valve inside me, relieving a pressure I'd grown accustomed to. When he woke up I was in the bathroom feeling bright, cleaning my contacts.

"It looks like noon," he said, turning my alarm clock toward him. It was a little past ten. "I like how your apartment gets a lot of light."

We walked to Bagel Nosh and ordered combo plates—bagel, eggs, sausage, hash browns, and lots of coffee. The diner was busy, crowded with the local Sunday brunch crowd. The mood was genial; even the stroller parents looked less harried, sedated by the warm weather. We got lucky and nabbed a booth in the corner. He drowned his hash browns in ketchup, his scrambled eggs in Tabasco sauce. He ate smiling, like the meal filled him with a pure delight. He'd had this same expression when he'd agreed to brunch, expectantly, like it was the only natural thing to do. His easy attitude made me queasy. I felt I was missing something, that there was a joke that I wasn't in on. I wanted to make him uncomfortable, to tease tight the space between us.

"I'm not sure why I had you stay last night," I said. When he looked up, I shrugged. "I mean I'm glad it happened, but it's not something I've done for a while."

"Me neither," he said. "I didn't think I'd get to see you again."

"You don't seem like you're that much younger. I mean maybe in some ways, but not others. Once we were alone you seemed different." I paused. "I had fun."

"Thanks," he said, almost blushing. "Me too."

He was both easygoing and unsure, and I was drawn to this cleaving in his character. I wondered how disappointment might change the shape of his face. I pictured his jaw tensed, his brow hardened and furrowed. This would make him look more self-assured, more adult, though maybe his eyes would still give him away. There was a daring vulnerability in the way he looked at me, like he'd never been hurt but was willing to go through the experience if necessary. I got the sense he believed even the worst would be more exciting than painful. I accidentally bumped his knee with mine, then bumped it again on purpose and left it there, our legs touching.

We left the diner in a light mood. The sun made us squint but also felt soothing, almost amniotic. When we got to where his car was parked on my block I thought he'd say goodbye, but he just followed me back into my apartment. We sat on the couch, facing the blank TV.

"We could watch a movie," I said.

We started kissing delicately. I wondered if we'd run out of things to say to each other, which made me grope at him more urgently. I kissed his eyelids, then gently pressed my teeth into the angular edges of his face. He pulled me to straddle him. I was wearing a wide V-neck T-shirt, and instead of taking it off, he pulled at the V, slipping his hands under it, exposing and kissing one breast, then the other. He breathed hard against my skin, dampening it, and I sensed he liked this little struggle with the shirt, having something he couldn't get too easily.

I got up and got a condom. I took off my pants, then straddled him again. I bit his ear as he entered me. He clenched his hands around my hips. When I looked at his face he had this look of wholesome desire, one that seemed clean and clearly defined and capable of fulfillment.

Suddenly I felt a sardonic sort of mirth. I wanted to slap him across his face. I could picture his shocked expression, then the expression loosening, until we both burst out laughing.

But I didn't. Instead I pushed his left cheek hard with my palm, turning his face so he couldn't see me, then kept his head pinned back against the couch. He didn't resist but his pulse quickened. For a second I felt chastened by his passivity, but then I just pushed his face harder.

Afterwards we lazily peeled the rest of our clothes off each other, then lay in a loose cuddle on the couch. The balcony doors were open but the white translucent curtains drawn; they billowed in and curdled gently in the breeze. We listened to the teenager next door with his basketball on the driveway, two quick bounces each time, followed by a lonely thump off the backboard.

Matt called that night. We breathed excitedly on our respective ends of the line, our minds patting around for things to talk about. "Tell me about you," I said, and he did so with enthusiasm, like he was happy to be asked at an interview the very question he'd diligently prepared for.

He'd grown up in Hancock Park, where his parents still lived. His father was a lawyer, his mother a psychotherapist. As he talked I imagined him as a child sitting next to his mother on a large couch, his feet dangling over the dark hardwood floors. He was telling her a story, a playground tale about a falling out with a friend, using a tone that showed he'd rehearsed the speech in his head, owning up to the part he played in the affair in the constructive way he'd been taught by his parents. This was the tone he was using now. He said his last relationship had been pretty shallow, though he hadn't realized it at the time. He said this carefully, like he wanted to be respectful and fair about what had happened, though I was left with the sense he was just recasting an insignificant college fling, the kind that didn't really go anywhere due to self-consciousness and peer pressure.

I tried to picture us walking hand-in-hand, together amidst throngs of people shopping in the city's main drags. I wondered how he might appear to me then. I remembered how his head had looked forced against the couch, how his eyes had stayed pressed shut like he was afraid of waking up. I pictured him now with his eyes closed, his cheek soft against the phone, his lips rounding delicately through the vowels. The image endeared him to me.

On Tuesday we went to see a movie, something I'd never done with Blake. Matt seemed to like the ritual of it, agreeing on a drama, finding a parking spot, picking out snacks. By the time we got through the concession line we were late, and we laughed as we ran up the escalators to the theater. Afterwards we rode down more sedately; the film had a sudden, depressing ending. When we pushed out the doors into the street, the night was dark but busy, full of lights and bright-eyed people, pleased to be moving about like we were all part of some bigger event. He suggested we walk to a nearby Italian restaurant-bar for a drink in a way that made me think he'd planned this beforehand. I squeezed his hand.

We sat at a small table; the seats at the bar in the corner were taken up by the regulars who all seemed to know each other, all middle-aged. They looked well-inebriated, jolly in a somewhat lethargic way, like they were resigned to the meager role they played in the small social circle of this bar for the rest of their lives.

"We're the youngest people here," Matt said. He laughed. "Sorry."

"I like it. We can actually hear each other."

At this he nodded approvingly. The wine arrived. He complimented what I was wearing and said I seemed different in a dress. I pointed at my heels. I was almost as tall as him in them. He told me his ex and he had been the exact same height. I asked him if that had bothered him and he said no, but that we fit better. I asked in what way and he flushed, then apologized for having brought up his ex again. "I don't know why I do that. I really don't think about her." He shook his head. "You can tell me about your ex, if you want."

"That's okay," I said.

"No really, it would make me feel better."

"It's really not worth mentioning."

He seemed flustered by this, but recovered. "Okay," he said, grinning. "Tell me something else about you."

"Like what?"

"Anything."

All the life facts I could think to mention seemed like landmines I'd been gingerly stepping around for years. The father who'd disappeared when I was seven. The mother who still worked for an hourly wage at the flower market. Even my friendships were too petty to mention. There were the college roommates whose emails I'd been avoiding in an effort to forget those messy, degrading years. And then there was Erin, with her new drunken hookup habit, each tryst followed by despondence, then resentment. We were a lot alike, except she expected better.

I put on my most enigmatic smile. "I can't think of anything under pressure," I said.

He leaned in, about to press me, but I turned and motioned for another round. When I looked back at him he grabbed my hand under the table and held it possessively with both hands. We grinned at each other. He asked me if I wanted to go to his place. First he said he wanted me to meet his roommate, a friend from college called Johnny, then said Johnny worked late at his startup most nights when I demurred.

We walked into a pitch-dark apartment. When Matt turned on the light, I saw the place was nothing like I'd imagined. The living room was neat and thoughtfully furnished, if somewhat cheaply, with well-matched secondhand furniture that gave the place a warm, welcoming feel.

"It's kind of like my place, but bigger," I said.

"Not with two people."

He led the way to his bedroom. His laptop's screensaver rotated through photos of Versailles; I asked to see other pictures from his trip. We sat shoulder to shoulder against the headboard, the computer shared across our knees. Most of the photos were of architecture. When we got to Italy a girl with sandy blond hair started popping up. Eventually there was one of Matt and the girl with their arms around each other. They were the same height and looked like fraternal twins. She was kissing his cheek.

Matt sighed. "I thought I deleted this." He stopped scrolling and faced me, like he owed me an explanation. He said they'd met in Venice. "The hostels were all like eight beds to a room," he said, "so we never had any real privacy. I think it felt more intense than it was, just because we were both all alone, in this extreme situation moving around every day."

I took over the touchpad and studied the photo. I noticed how young he looked, like a kid on spring break. "You look happy," I said.

"We emailed for a while, but she lives in Sydney," he said. "That was the thing. She acted like she knew what she wanted, but she didn't. She was so—the girls my age—" I looked at him. He had on a perplexed grimace that seemed put on to mask something else. Then he suddenly laughed. He squeezed the sides of his head with his hands. "Okay, this is so not like me," he said. "No more ex talk from now on, I promise."

I laughed. "It's fine," I said. "Really."

"Now you really have to tell me something about your ex. The mysterious guy with the tie you won't talk about."

I paused. "Hey, I'm really not seeing him anymore."

"I know," he said. He got up and put the laptop on the desk. "I'm just curious because you're all secretive about it."

"I'll tell you some stories next time," I said. I took his wrist and pulled him. "You've been warned."

He started tickling me and I shrieked. Just then we heard the front door open; Johnny was home. "Shhhh," Matt said, putting a finger on my lips. "We have to be quiet." He slid his body over mine, pinning me down. "Or else my roommate might call the cops."

We lay still, holding our breaths, until Johnny's steps disappeared into his room. Then Matt reached up and turned off the lamp. He had blackout curtains; we could only locate each other by touch. We took our clothes off slowly, piece by piece, then had hushed, exploratory sex over the covers. The quiet of it felt a little like college, and the unhurried pleasure nothing like it at all.

The next morning, though, when Matt's alarm went off at five for his opening shift, I woke up gloomy and angry. Our stopping in at the bar in itself seemed a juvenile act, embarrassing in its desperation to interact as an adult couple. When Matt dropped me off I dozed for a bit, then went to Bagel Nosh to try working there; I'd seen a new "Free WiFi" sign on the door. I hid irritably behind my laptop, but no one was paying me any attention anyway. Only a few people were in the place, all older men in their late fifties or sixties, each sitting at his own table, sopping up runny egg yolk with bagel bits and watching golf on the TV. They looked like they'd been divorced for years, comfortably resigned. I imagined their female counterparts, how they must be eating similar meals, but alone in their homes. I could easily imagine myself as one of these women, a thought that troubled me. Blake would never end up here in middle age. He'd find a willing new woman right away, younger and more docile. And Matt—he wouldn't get divorced. His wife would outlive him, plan a warm memorial service where friends would weep genuinely and fondly then leave comforted, with a sense they'd communed, if briefly, with the delicate beauty of the cycle of life.

I thought about what Erin would say if she knew I was seeing Matt. These days she was too often in her sullen post-hookup, bubble-burst mood to be happy for me. I imagined myself breaking the news in different tones: an excited whisper, a matter-of-fact summary, a preoccupied aside. In each case her reaction would be exactly the same, a tight smile, vaguely tinged with jealousy. I pictured her nodding with that forced grin as I talked about him, then saying something benign on the surface but cutting beneath, something like, "So when's the next keg party," before turning back to her drink. I let myself feel the sting of this remark, feel it spread from my center like a thick fog. This made me feel closer to Matt, united against a common adversary. I felt protective of him again, his amiable sincerity.

I ate my hash browns. They tasted greasier than usual, like they were cooked in old oil. The TV was showing highlights from the US Open. A golfer who had Blake's posture took a big swing. The ball launched, and the camera cut to the golfer's face, showed how it shifted into a satisfied smirk even before the ball started its downward arc.

We'd made plans for Saturday night, but when Matt called after his shift ended on Friday I invited him over. I thought seeing him might bring back the sense of playful complicity. "Missed me?"

he said when I opened the door. He presented me with a cookie, one of the artisanal ones from the coffee shop with its dime-sized dollops of dark chocolate, and a pound of Yirgacheffe. He hesitated until I smiled, then he leaned in and kissed me. He tasted like café au lait. He pushed the door closed with his elbow and pulled me against him.

"Have you had dinner?" I asked.

We walked to Whole Foods. His mood was buoyant. He wanted to try everything in the hot food section and filled his container with a weird mishmash of Indian and Greek dishes, plus mac and cheese. Watching him do this, I felt a sense of revulsion grow, though the rational part of me thought his impulse to get the variety he wanted was wise, the true point of buffet-style dining, in fact. I looked down at my meager meal of salmon and rice. I added charred broccoli, then mashed potatoes, then a half-slice of lasagna.

Once we were back at my apartment and the wine was opened, his enthusiasm felt more touching. We drank in gulps and ate our dinners happily, sitting thigh to thigh on the couch. It felt like we were in collusion again, though when I tried to get a good grip on that feeling I felt it go slack. We seemed to be miming togetherness, showing off our united resolve in an attempt to scare off a force that didn't even exist.

"Next time, we should pack up all this stuff and have a picnic," Matt said. "Like at the Hollywood Bowl."

"Okay," I said. "I haven't been there since I went to see Björk three years ago. Nosebleed seats, but it was fun."

"My parents actually have season tickets to the classical series. One of the boxes up front."

I nodded. I imagined him asking his parents for the tickets. Then I imagined him stealing them, slipping them out of his mother's red planner on his way out the door. I couldn't decide how I'd feel about this, whether I'd like the cheeky exuberance or scorn it, but I could see us there, sitting in the center box with our Whole Foods containers and plastic forks, eating self-consciously under the curious gaze of the gray-haired couples sitting around us, staring as they carefully masticated their cobb salads with their dentures.

To change the subject I put my head on his shoulder, then leaned my whole body heavily against him. He pressed back and started gently mussing my hair. He said one of the actresses in the movie we'd seen, the brunette that played the star's sadistic sister, had come in to the coffee shop that day. She'd ordered a macchiato, then asked for more milk. "She seemed nice," he said. Then politely, he asked about my work. I said I was getting burned out, that the work was steady, but repetitive. I said I was thinking of working in-house again, though not for tiny trades like I'd done before. I wanted to be somewhere I could be proud of, ideally at one of the big Condé Nast magazines, though that might be unrealistic unless I was willing to take a major pay cut and fetch coffee. Still, I wanted to try living in Manhattan before I got too old.

"A part of me thinks I'm still running away from my problems," I said, "but I've been back in LA for a while now and still nothing's holding me here."

He was quiet for a minute, then said, "Are you saying I'm a problem?"

I was surprised by this. "Of course not," I said. "This has nothing to do with you." I paused. "Haven't you ever wanted to live anywhere besides LA?"

"I traveled all last year," he said.

I was about to say that wasn't the same thing as living somewhere else, but I didn't think he'd be willing to acknowledge the difference. He wouldn't understand it. "That's true," I said. "You did." I shrugged, my shoulder nuzzling against his chest. "It's just a fantasy I have when I'm feeling bored with work."

This seemed to satisfy him. He collected my hair into a loose ponytail in his left hand, then massaged my shoulders. I turned my head and we kissed deeply. We kept kissing, him running his hands over my arms.

"This feels good," I said, and meant it. "It was never like this with my ex."

He stiffened. "What was it like?"

"Different," I said. "This is better. Like college, but better."

"What do you mean?" He laughed nervously. "How like college?"

I leaned in again but he pulled back, still smiling. "You owe me a story. You promised," he said. I rolled my eyes. I turned my face forward, away from him. He started caressing my arms again. "Tell me," he said.

I hesitated, but then started in. "My ex—he was really more of a fuck buddy if I'm being really honest about it," I said. "He worked at a financial firm, always busy, so we'd basically just meet up to have sex."

Already, his hands felt more rigid.

"He lived in this condo in Venice, fourth floor, overlooking the beach. This one time when I walked in he was on the balcony, clipping his nails. So we did it there. He didn't even take off his jacket, like he didn't have the time. It was dark but there were these surfer kids by the water that I thought were watching us. I told him we were going to end up on YouTube but he said people couldn't see if the lights were off."

"Were they?"

I couldn't tell if his tone was anxious or angry. "My point is, it wasn't a good relationship, or even a relationship. We barely talked and when we did it was like we were just trying to one-up each other. The sex was like that too. By the end, anyway."

He was quiet. He'd stopped moving his hands. They were folded neatly, one on top of the other, just above my belly button.

"Hey," I said. I turned my body and burrowed my face into the crevice of his neck. "Are you okay?"

"Why wouldn't I be?"

I propped myself up on an elbow. His face was a scrabble of antipathy and dejection, though I could tell a small part of him was still struggling to shrug it off. He shifted his eyes to look at me. I kissed him and he kissed me back, reluctantly, then forcefully.

His manner changed. He turned so I was beneath him on the couch. He was simulating a sudden passion but I could feel a violence beneath it. Suddenly, I could taste his teeth. His body seemed bonier, pressing down on me like a dull weapon. He shoved his hand down my pants. His fingers felt cold and severe. He turned his hand and roughly ground his knuckles into me. "Ow," I said. "Careful." He said sorry under his breath, then unzipped my pants and did it again, a bit more gently. He tugged at my hair, gripping it near the roots; the pull wasn't hard, but I found myself growing afraid.

"Matt, stop," I said.

"What's wrong?" he said. I pushed his chest and he sat up. He scraped his hands through his hair then exhaled, a loose sigh. He turned his head to look at me.

The space between us felt precarious. "You were hurting me," I said.

"Really?"

His expression was hard but uncertain, like he was trying to decide whether to be apologetic or angry. He watched me zip up and straighten my clothes. Then he took my hand. I let it hang limply in his palm.

"I'm sorry," he said. "I thought we were having fun."

I got up and took the deli containers to the kitchen, then stayed there for a minute, breathing deeply.

When I came back Matt was still in the same position, seated with his feet on the floor, his left hand extended to where he'd been holding mine. "Are we fighting?" he said.

"No." I stood there, on the other side of the coffee table. "I don't know."

"I thought it was what you wanted."

I looked down at my feet. The nail polish on my left big toe was slightly chipped, had been since the coffee shop date with Blake. He'd pointed this out as soon as he saw it, when I'd finished the latte and we'd stood up to leave. "If you can't even paint them properly, what's the fucking point?" he'd said. "Why draw attention to something ugly?" He'd stomped out in front of me, his expensive loafers doing their confident heel-toe heel-toe away. It was then that I first noticed the coarseness of my feet, their pudgy stubbiness. The discovery was painful, but also had a cleansing, illuminating quality. I marveled at how I'd never noticed this before, how no one else had had the blunt honesty to point out this obvious fact about my feet to me. That was when, I think, I finally began to accept it wouldn't ever happen with Blake, that it was time to give up on my self-improvement project. I could lose some weight and repaint my toes, sure. But I'd never be able to change the shape of my feet.

I realized Matt had said something but that I hadn't heard it. I looked up. "What?" I said.

"It feels like you want me to leave."

I looked at my feet again, curling my toes under. "It's not that," I said. I could feel his eyes on me, though I didn't look at him. He sat there, breathing audibly. I remembered the way his slack, sleeping body had looked, swaddled in sheets. The memory was so exact I could tilt and shift it in my mind, examine it from different angles. There was something about his splayed posture that looked like yearning, even in its helplessness, that hinted at some tangible pleasure between us, even if incoherent and messy.

"I'm sorry," I said. "I'm not good at telling stories."

I met his eyes. The curtains shivered. The chilled breeze was uncomfortable, but consoling too, how it prickled the skin in its predictable way.

Holiday Love Scarf

My friend Matt was a Sagittarius. For his twenty-fifth birthday, he invited everyone he knew on Facebook to a comedy show at Largo, followed by drinks. Per Matt's insistence, I ended up carpooling from Santa Monica with two friends of his I hadn't met before—Christian, a recent grad school dropout who drove with his angular face set in self-absorbed silence, and Danielle, a project coordinator for a national environmental nonprofit. Danielle was a young, heavy girl whose angry brown eyes contradicted the childlike lilt of her voice. For most of the drive, she spoke urgently about the harmful effects of BPA on human reproduction, occasionally dropping her voice to make jarring sexual innuendos about sperm motility. She acted horrified at the mini bottle of Aquafina in my purse. "All those plastic toxins—It's really not something you can afford to do to your body, at your age," she said, then quickly added, "Our age, I mean."

I was thirty-two. "It's okay," I said. "The planet could use fewer kids."

Danielle took a big inhale, but Christian preempted her by pulling into the parking lot. He offered to pay but we both handed him fivers.

The comedy show was a strange mix of droll and slapstick humor. It went by quickly, and the crowd walked en masse to the dim, speakeasy-style bar next door known for its complicated and expensive cocktails. I started a conversation with the woman next to me, Natalie, who said she was going to visit her mother in San Diego for the holidays, but that she wasn't looking forward to it.

"My boyfriend got me a book, *Codependent No More*," she said. "It's not that my mom's ever forced me to do anything, but I've always felt obligated."

She sounded vaguely wistful. I told her that my mother used to pepper me with small, passive-aggressive insults about my appearance when I saw her, but that things were easier now that she'd remarried and moved back to Korea.

"I miss her sometimes, but I have to admit I'm happier during the holidays," I said.

Danielle, who I didn't realize had been listening, piped in. "So what are you doing for Christmas?"

"This kind of stuff," I said, gesturing in a circle to signify the evening.

"Don't you have any other family?" There was her horrified tone again.

I ignored her. "I'll be back," I said to Natalie. "I'm going to buy the birthday boy a drink."

Matt and I had dated briefly when we'd first met a few years before. It hadn't worked out, but due mostly to his good nature we'd unexpectedly become pretty good friends, the kind that shared dating woes. He'd recently had a couple brief affairs with married women. The experiences had left him feeling jilted, though he'd been the one to end things. The women had seemed too glad to see him go.

"You said they weren't really your type physically and had too much emotional baggage," I said.

"It's that they never even considered leaving," he said. "Not even on a fantasy level."

"Can't you ever just have fun?"

Matt always went for strong, independent women, a commendable trait, but after landing one he'd glom onto her in a cloying, wheedling way until she inevitably decided she was better off alone. Then he'd call me to rehash what happened, cataloguing the timeline of the relationship in the listless tone of existential writers before starting to whine self-pityingly. Whenever he did this I'd want to slap him and tell him to grow a pair, then would feel guilty and suggest going out for ice cream. His favorite flavor was mint chocolate chip.

This night Matt was at the center of a dozen or so of his coworkers who'd formed a possessive circle around him, busy rehashing the show. I saw Matt was holding a full drink already, and so made my way to the bar to get a drink just for myself.

People ebbed and flowed, ignoring me. After a while, Natalie came to stand by the bar too. "I wasn't going to come when my boyfriend canceled," she said. "But I'm glad I did. I liked what you said about your mother."

"You mean we're both codependent?" I said, aggrieved.

"No, no," she said. "I have this friend who just had a baby. She moved to Simi Valley, had no one to talk to, so I drove up to visit her just to be nice. Then when I got there, she started making fun of the way some people dress, and halfway through, I realized she was talking about me."

"Did you say something?"

"No, but I wish I had." She sighed. "It's a process. Baby steps."

Her expression was more resigned than hopeful. I noticed she was dressed very chicly, with expensive leather boots and an oversized knitted scarf. I asked her where she'd gotten the scarf and she said she sold it at her boutique in Santa Monica. "We're neighbors," I said, and she gave me a ride home.

The next afternoon, driving, I called Matt. I hadn't gotten to talk to him much at the bar, and had left early, which I felt guilty about; he tended to take little things personally. But he sounded happy to hear from me.

"So what did you think?" he said.

"He was funny," I said. "I liked the joke about the paleo—"

"No, no, I mean, about Christian. He's wanted to meet you since he saw that picture of you on Facebook. The one from Halloween, where you're hitting me with a ruler."

I'd dressed up as a sexy school teacher—tight blouse, cat-eye glasses, and a flashy copy of *Flesh Unlimited*. The ruler had been my bookmark. "Really?" I said. "He barely said anything to me."

"He can be a little shy until you get to know him. He's really smart. He remembers everything, and he speaks French. In grad school he was studying this crazy photographer, Hippolyte—"

"Is he unemployed?"

"He has a second interview at this architecture firm."

I agreed to go out with him, then hanging up, felt disgruntled that the one guy interested in me was jobless, lost and floundering in his thirties. I tried to remember what Christian looked like in more detail. When he'd smiled I'd noticed his nice teeth, and in my memory the angularity of his face grew more definite until his expression turned confident, knowing. An architecture firm sounded cool, I thought.

I parked at a meter and went into Chado Tea Room. I was there for a writers and publicists roundtable; the idea was to bring the two sides together to talk out how to help each other. It was an informal thing organized by the editor of a health newsletter that I wrote for regularly. As I'd expected, the meeting was all women, a dozen of them, the PR agents dressed smartly, the writers more dowdily in bulky jeans. I sat down and ordered a maple scone. The two women near me introduced themselves, then went back to talking about a male restaurateur they despised.

"And then he told my friend he would've gone home with me if he wasn't already seeing someone."

"Seriously?"

"It's like he can't conceive of the idea that I might not be attracted to him."

"He's so handsy too."

I tried to join in. "I knew a guy like that," I said. "I always wanted to tell him off, but when you do, they think you're flirting with them."

"So what did you do?" The first one asked curiously.

"Nothing," I said.

"But then they'll go around telling people you're into them."

"They'll do that regardless."

"True." The woman looked vexed and thoughtful; her eyes were filled with angry idealism. She was in her early twenties, the baby fat on her cheeks adorable against the serious set of her jaw. It felt sweet that she thought this wrong could somehow be righted. In fact, her mood was infectious. By the time I was on my way home, I found myself twitchy with a vague sense of agency, that if I thought about it hard enough, I could find a way to tweak the world a little for the better. It was rush hour. Dejected drivers were changing lanes too often, further stalling the traffic. I imagined opening my windows and yelling out, "Don't you see what you're doing?" then let the thought slowly dissipate, along with the empowered mood. The phone rang.

"I wasn't sure when would be a good time to call." It was Christian. "Matt said you work sporadically."

He sounded different than I remembered, calmer, which made me unexpectedly nervous. I felt as if we were riding up an escalator, he a step above me and looking down while I craned my neck up suppliantly. I wanted to bring us back into equilibrium.

"Matt said you liked that picture of me hitting him," I said.

"Huh?" he said, then laughed briefly. "Well, it's the first picture I saw of you. Look, I know it's a little weird. I was going to say something last night but that Danielle girl talked our ears off, and then I turned around and you were gone." His tone turned gentle. "I'm really not a creepy person. Matt can vouch for me."

I tried to match his tone, but it came out petulant and warbly. The anxious part of me still wanted to make him uncomfortable. "I don't know anything about you," I said. "What kind of work do you do?"

"Actually, I just got a new job," he said quickly, "starting Monday. I mean, I still have to call them back, but they've made the offer." He breathed in sharply. "I thought maybe I could take you out this weekend and we could celebrate."

I found the slight nervous pause in his speech charming. I immediately accepted. This seemed to have the effect of either repelling or disorienting him; he got off the phone quickly, saying he'd text with the details. His sudden desertion turned me morose and apathetic. I drove glumly, resigned to the traffic, resentful that the guys I met showed only cold arrogance and flaccid inhibition, never anything in between.

I decided to call my friend Erin at work. Usually, Erin was my favorite wingwoman, though I'd known better than to ask her to go to Matt's party. Erin disliked Matt. The night I'd met him, I'd left the bar with him, abandoning Erin. In my defense she'd been busy making out with a guy that she ended up taking home that night too. But that guy had never called Erin again, while Matt had stuck around. For that, she was bitter, and she took it out on Matt, though she wasn't really a vengeful person, just glum of late. When she picked up, she seemed glad for the interruption; her voice had that efficient, workplace tone, tempered with a brooding angst. I could see her in her plastic office at the bank, her hair pinned efficiently away from her face, her feet shifting slightly in her heels as she powered through her files. She said her work always felt satisfying when she was in it, but hollow when dissected in retrospect. To cheer her up I suggested that she leave work early and we go holiday shopping, just for ourselves. I gave her the address of Natalie's boutique.

The boutique was a cute, little place on Montana Avenue, an upscale shopping street. Several slim, well-heeled women browsed, their faces grim and determined, as if from the effort of keeping their weight down through middle age. When we walked in, Erin and Natalie took to each other immediately. They quickly began bemoaning the dating scene in LA. Natalie said she'd met her boyfriend through OKCupid, and encouraged us to try it too.

"I've had to retrain myself completely," she said, "to actually make this relationship work."

Natalie's tone was encouraging, but I suddenly felt weary. The conversation sounded very familiar. I said I'd tried online dating before, and that it hadn't gone well. But Erin's face turned eager; she asked Natalie what she meant. Natalie said in the past she used to do nice things for her boyfriends, only to find herself taken for granted, then cast aside. "I'd be like, 'I got a present for you,'" Natalie said, using a doofy, cartoon character voice while shuffling toward us in a silly, weeble-wobble walk, her arms outstretched like she was offering up a gift. "But he should be the one giving me gifts. I didn't realize it, but I was emasculating them. I was totally sabotaging myself." She recommended a relationship course that she'd taken, a series of online seminars, starting with one about bringing love into your life, which she said outlined concrete steps you could take to get guys to pay attention to you and ask you out. One of these methods consisted of catching a guy's eye and holding it for five full seconds.

"It really works!" she said. "I mean, I'd met my boyfriend already when I took it, but my friend who took it with me said it's like magic. They'll get up out of their seat walk over from all the way around the bar and offer to buy you a drink."

"Meeting guys isn't the issue," I said. "It's everything else."

But Erin's eyes were glittering. She listened to Natalie, rapt, lit up by the winter sunlight, which had refracted through a window and was dappling her face with dots of iridescent color. When she tilted her head down slightly the spots moved into her hair, covered it like jeweled netting. Looking at her, I thought she was radiant, and wondered why she always seemed to have such a hard go of it, with the guys. I wondered why I did too. Natalie promised to email us a link to the seminar website. Before we left Erin and I both bought scarves—I got two, one to send to my sister in Portland—the same style but different colors from the one Natalie was wearing the night before. Natalie sold them to us at half price, and when we said that was too generous she said it was fine and smiled shyly, her teeth peeking out meekly between her lips.

I had a good week, a productive one, the days running in a neat little seam. A couple nights, I met Erin for happy hour. She was cheerier; she'd signed up for the seminar Natalie had recommended, and was anxious for it to begin. I didn't tell her about Christian but her enthusiasm lit a pilot light of hope in me too. I could sense it in my quiet moments, blue and steady and waiting.

For the date I dressed in monochrome—black pants, black heels, black coat, plus the new black-and-white scarf from Natalie's shop hung around my neck in loose coils. The outfit looked stereotypically New York and made me feel protected, like I was encased in an urban shield denoting self-sufficiency. I tried putting my hair up in a bun but it made me look too severe, so I left it down and added earrings, big silver hoops that I thought lent me a more receptive flair.

I got to the coffee shop a few minutes early, but Christian was already there, sitting at a good spot in the back away from the foot traffic. When I walked in the door he raised his hand in greeting and stood up. His light brown hair was loosely styled away from his face. He wore dark jeans and a black moto jacket that looked expensive but old. He had the kind of good posture that made me aware of my own; I noticed myself straightening my shoulders as I walked toward him. I was about to shake his hand when he caught me in a quick hug, then we sat down. He asked me if he could get me something to drink, but there was a long line at the counter, so I said I'd wait. "You can have my tea if you want," he said tentatively. "I haven't touched it yet."

I declined, thanking him. He said he would have liked to have taken me out to dinner, but that he wasn't sure if it would have made me uncomfortable, that kind of time commitment. I shrugged, then smiled. I said I was thinking about getting a hot chocolate.

"Because we could still go to a restaurant," he said. "If you want."

I was about to shake my head, then remembered what Natalie said about emasculation. "I'd like that," I said hurriedly. "I mean, we should celebrate your new job! Dessert, wine." I suddenly stopped, anxious that I'd raised the bar too high on the dinner, made it too expensive.

"Do you like tapas?" he asked.

"Absolutely," I said. I was grinning unnaturally; when I realized this I abruptly remolded my face into a neutral expression. Then we smiled awkwardly at each other.

"Me too. I think I was a Spaniard in a former life." He turned serious. "Wait, I didn't really mean that. I don't believe in re-incarnation." He looked at me intently as he said this, like he wanted reassurance that I wasn't a reincarnationist either. I laughed to show that I wasn't, then felt annoyed with myself. My reaction seemed too suppliant.

He drank his tea in a gulp, then we jaywalked across the street to the tapas restaurant. The place had recently reopened with a sleeker look, ebony tables and warm, ruddy lighting. It was packed but we got seats at the bar. Next to us a man ate alone, attacking his cheese plate with vicious little bites. Between pokes at his phone he snuck glances at us with a timid envy that made me feel lucky to be with a date. I glanced at the menu, then when Christian asked what I wanted, suggested that he order for us, he being a former Spaniard and all. This seemed to imbue him with a small, glowing pleasure. He took on the task with enthusiasm, conferring energetically with the waiter over taste profiles of the cured meats. He sampled two different wines before settling on a third. Then he turned back to me.

"It's weird because Matt's told me so much about you already," he said. "I don't know where to start."

I asked him about himself. He'd grown up in Ohio, the baby of the family. His mother raised him like a little prince, he said, and he was close to his parents now, though he disagreed with them on everything; they listened to Glenn Beck and got into pyramid schemes. His older sister had four kids, one of them autistic. He was the black sheep, he said. He'd gone to college in Iowa, then moved out to Los Angeles on a whim, first working as a PA at Warner Bros., then bouncing through odd jobs before starting an MA program in creative writing at Cal State Northridge. "To clear my head," he said.

I noticed he said the words "odd jobs" with an ironic gloss, as if he was protecting me from the dark and outré details of his life until he knew I was ready for them. His tone grew more relaxed as he spoke, prouder, like he was happy for the opportunity to shape the vague meanderings of his life into concrete proof of an adventurous spirit. He said he'd traveled to Thailand twice in the last year. His eagerness to be perceived as a rebel of sorts roused my sardonic proclivities—he actually used the word hedonist to describe himself—yet that same eagerness also revealed a vulnerability in him that softened me. I wondered if I talked the same way about my life, if my little attempts to reframe my past were similarly transparent and frantic.

When the food arrived it was clear Christian had ordered way too much. We played Tangram with the waiter, trying to get the tiny plates to fit into our bar space.

I asked about the architecture firm. Christian looked confused at first, then said Matt had misinterpreted, the job was at a nonprofit developer for low-income housing. His title, which he seemed satisfied about, was Director of Outreach. "Basically the liaison between the public and the nonprofit," he said.

As we talked we shared the food gingerly, careful not to clash opinions or forks. At one point he lifted his glass of wine, then realized it was empty and set it back down. The bartender quickly came over but Christian waved him away after seeing my full glass; I'd forgotten about it in my nervousness. I started sipping industriously. He said it must take a lot of discipline to work as a freelance writer, that that kind of self-imposed structure didn't come naturally to him, which was one reason he'd left grad school. He said this in a way that hinted he had a certain disdain for routine, its lack of passion. I watched him talk, imagining how he'd looked at CSUN, the class discussing Lolita's agency while he sat in the back, agitated with the quiet bookishness of it all. He said he'd read some of my articles, googled them. He liked one I'd written about a raw juice cleanse I'd done, that what I'd described was exactly how he'd felt on a similar cleanse.

"Those types of articles are just repackaged PR pitches," I said. "The so-called benefits—they're really placebo effects."

I'd meant to be humbly self-deprecating, but my tone came out huffy and caught him off guard. "Well, I agree with the stuff about it curing cancer being unlikely," he said quickly. "But I did feel cleaner afterwards—"

"Starvation will do that to you," I said. The words were still harsher than I'd wanted but this time I managed to sound more teasing.

He smiled. "So that's what that was," he said. He turned thoughtful, turning over a piece of beet to better pincer it. "The way some people talk about juicing, you realize they're actually obsessive-compulsive, or have an eating disorder. But there's something about their obsessiveness that makes me want to get into it too."

"I agree," I said. "The extremeness of it. It gives you a sort of focus."

"So we have something in common," he said. The bartender came over again and Christian gave him a nod this time, for a second glass. "You look very—professional today. Is this how you usually dress? I mean, I like it." He said that last part quickly, which made it unconvincing.

I got home close to eleven, feeling like the date had gone well enough yet fettered with an undercurrent of apprehension, like I'd done something wrong but couldn't put a finger on what that mistake was yet. I went to bed immediately to sleep away the feeling, and woke up near dawn, spent from the rushed confusion of my dreams.

It was the Sunday before Christmas. I spent it at a Korean spa with Erin, then in the early evening, when Christian called, told him about it. There had been a minor kerfuffle at the beginning when Erin tried to wear a bikini into the hot tub; her argument for the tired-looking staff was that a different Korean spa had allowed her to do so. In the end, she got naked, but was angry for a while; I had stayed out of the fight, which she seemed to see as a kind of betrayal. After the sauna, though, she got over it. I'd noticed that most of the women arrived alone, going about their soak-and-scrub routines in a vigorous and somewhat grim, business-like fashion, before pulling on the shapeless regulation loungewear and padding off to nap in the heated room, splayed out unabashedly with their mouths open. I mimicked them, and woke up feeling discombobulated and puffy.

Christian had had a long conversation with his parents, who were hurt he wasn't coming home for the holidays. It was the first Christmas he wasn't spending with them. The year before he'd flown back with his girlfriend at the time, a woman five years older than him, whom his parents had loved, thinking her a calming influence. Christian and the girl had broken up shortly after that, but his parents brought her up again that day, which had led to an argument.

"I think we stayed together so long because we were just that age, when people couple up," he said. I didn't ask how long. "It's weird, she never mentioned kids when we were dating, but when we finally broke up she gave me all this crap about how I'd robbed away her last chance of having a baby and left me with nothing. It made me think all women are the same."

"Well, it's an easy argument to make," I said.

"That all women just want to have babies?"

"No. I'm saying maybe she didn't want the relationship to end, or was feeling wounded, and the whole baby thing was the first thing she could think of to make you feel shitty." I paused. "Though, who knows?" I added. "You knew her, not me."

There was an angry silence while he considered this. Then he asked if I'd had dinner.

Christian lived in the Fairfax district, in a one-bedroom that was fairly spacious but looked cheap, with popcorn ceilings and pinkish carpet mottled with faint stains. The hodgepodge furniture looked assembled from garage sales. When I arrived the apartment was filled with the pungent aroma of prunes and olives and garlic, mingled with the bouquet of decanting wines. He'd cooked enough for an army—homemade hummus, a dense black quinoa and avocado salad, and a gigantic casserole dish of chicken Marbella. He'd mentioned that he enjoyed cooking, but seeing the spread, I was duly impressed. He told me, more convincingly this time, that he liked my dress, a simple scoop-neck I'd changed into self-consciously.

We sat down at one end of his too-big dining table, the five other chairs staring us down. Once we started eating, he became more spirited. He asked me if I liked the wine, and when I said I did, said he'd made it himself. "It's my second year," he said. "It's more acidic than I'd like, but I know how to correct for that now."

I noticed the wine cooler buzzing in the corner, and next to it, a barrel-shaped contraption with vinyl tubing and a red cork-er balanced on top. He said winemaking had become a semi-serious hobby. He was planning to get his sommelier's license, and had just started a blog.

"It's not as hard as you'd think," he said. "And a lot of fun. I drive upstate to pick the grapes at this one vineyard. Though next year, I'd like to make that trip with someone."

I didn't know how to respond. "Your ex wasn't into it?"

"No," he said, then shook his head. "Definitely not." He broke apart a roll into tiny, deliberate pieces before starting to eat it. "It dragged on far too long as it was. Honestly, it started falling apart as soon as we moved in together."

I nodded.

"You know those intense, obsessive relationships, where your lives get tangled up immediately? It was one of those."

He said he had a tendency to let things move too fast. "I think I saw her as a wounded bird I could protect somehow. But we both took that too far. By the time we broke up there was no way we could be friends. The last time we talked, I was at the grocery store. She called me and started screaming at me about how I shouldn't leave without telling her where I was going, that she needed to know where I was, at all times, basically." He looked up from his plate at me. Something in my face made him change course. "That's what I think is great about you and Matt. That you stayed friends. Had that level of—maturity."

Gingerly, we started trading Matt stories. Christian explained how they'd met, at a pick-up soccer game in Westwood Park. I half-listened, grousing over what he'd said about his ex. I'd never had any intense, obsessive relationships. I wallowed in a mix of jealousy and contempt, the two feelings jostling each other for dominance like rancorous siblings. I felt like a box of cereal in an aisle full of cereal boxes, in a supermarket in a city with countless supermarkets, at a time when no one ate carbs. All the good things in life seemed to happen only through rare intersections of luck and timing, chance meetings that never happened for me. I thought about Matt getting a text from the plump married woman about how she understood completely, things had run their course. I pictured Natalie paging through her codependency book and carefully dogearing a page. I watched Christian's hands; he'd stopped eating the roll and was absent-mindedly playing with the remaining pieces until they disintegrated into crumbs.

"You've gotten really quiet," he said. He was studying me, his expression vaguely apprehensive and contrite. "I hope I didn't upset you."

"Upset me?" I said. I shook my head. "No, I'm just listening. I'm interested." I smiled, leaning forward. I wasn't sure if Christian was just a blithe kind of a guy who innocently, if obtusely, shared whatever came to mind, or if he was more deliberate, if the effect he'd produced on me was exactly what he'd been going for.

"I think I'm trying to be honest and up front, but going about it the wrong way. Like if I put it all out there . . ." He took a long sip of wine. "I practically dragged you over here tonight."

"I wanted to come." I said. This seemed to calm him. We looked at each other, and for a second I thought he was going to kiss me, but he didn't, so I kept talking. "I've met people like that. They seem like exactly what you've been looking for at the time. But then you realize you projected all this stuff onto them . . ."

He nodded. "It's been good in a way. I've gotten more cautious, not just always jumping into the next thing that comes along."

Somehow this elbowed awake that resentful, unlucky feeling again. No one ever took any leaps of faith for me. He saw me look at the clock. It was after eleven. "I talked the whole night," he said resignedly. I disagreed lightly, playing nice. We got up to clear the plates. I started running the water and he said it was okay, he would do the dishes in the morning, but seemed glad for it when I said I wanted to help—it was only fair since he'd cooked.

Standing at the sink together, he asked me about my past relationships. I said there hadn't been anything serious of late, that the last guy I dated was in the summer, and even that hadn't lasted long. He asked why not and I said ultimately, he hadn't made enough time for me. He asked what kind of time I considered appropriate. I laughed nervously. "I don't know," I said. "More than once a week?" He nodded, like he found this answer satisfying, doable. I found this appealing. The domestic act of washing dishes together drew me into his bubble and I realized I liked it there—this foreign, homey place. When we finished he suddenly leaned down and kissed me. He held my face in his hands; they were soft and clean from the dishwater.

We made out for a while, then went to his bedroom. We mussed around on his polyester bedspread. After a few minutes I told him I didn't want to have sex; I had my period. He said that was okay, he still wanted me to stay over, if I wanted. At that it was like it was decided. We groped at each other slowly and ardently, occasionally freeing each other of another piece of clothing, until what seemed like hours later, we were both naked except for our underwear. We rolled around hotly, not having sex. He seemed more confident now, firm, like in bed he was comfortable being his true self. Eventually he put his hand between my legs and touched me over my panties until I came. Afterwards I started giving him a hand job, then watched him masturbate, on his knees straddling my body, until he came on my chest. He wiped me down with a warm, damp washcloth.

We got under the covers. We started kissing again, more gently this time, but pressed hard against each other. With his thumb he caressed my eyebrow, then my ear. "I really like you," he said. "I want you to know, the other women I'd been seeing, I've told them I met someone, I'm not going to see them anymore." As he said this he was looking away slightly, like a child that had told a tall tale he'd almost convinced himself was true. I felt an uncomfortable mixture of empathy and derisive mirth. I suppose it wasn't out of the realm of possibility that he'd been dating a few other women, he was attractive enough, but something about the way he'd made this declaration made me disbelieve him. It seemed too spot-on a detail of the way he wanted to be seen—as someone unconventional and daring and profligate—and it felt desperate, beseeching in its effort to convince me that he was a catch and I the lucky one. In a way I did feel lucky. But I also wanted to call him on it. I like you too, I wanted to say. But you're not fooling anyone.

We dozed next to each other fitfully, the room humid with our body heat. I had a hard time falling asleep, and when I did, kept waking up. In this way, I didn't dream.

The next morning I drove Erin to the airport. She was going home for the holidays; her parents lived in New Jersey. During the drive, Erin discussed the relationship seminars. They didn't start until the New Year, but she had signed on to the website and watched some of the free mini videos, including one about online dating.

"Basically, we need to look at it as a numbers game, and just go out with a lot of people. And right away, too, so you're not all invested in someone before you even meet. None of this email-ing and talking on the phone for weeks." She leaned toward me.

"The magic number is thirty-seven." She sat back, then wagged her hand. "Or around there. You have to go out a lot."

Her expression was anticipatory, but with a disgruntled undercurrent, like she was aggravated about all the time she'd wasted before discovering these truths. Still, she seemed happier, more alert. She was wearing a crisp, blue crewneck and a high ponytail, which gave her the look of an unusually enthusiastic student, the kind that sat in the front row and raised her hand a lot.

"After the trip, I'm starting fresh," she said. "So while I'm at home I want to do like a cleanse. Vegan, no gluten. Mostly raw food. I need to reset my system. I'm not going to drink at all. Or if I do, only organic wine, no sulfites. Although I might go out with my friend Vanessa in New York for New Year's . . ." She ran mental calculations, negotiating with herself.

"Vanessa the alcoholic?" I asked.

"Well, yeah. Though I probably shouldn't have called her that, when you don't even know her. I don't know that she's really an alcoholic. It's just that whenever I go out with her I end up drinking way too much. Last time . . ." She came to an uneasy pause. "The thing is, I've been taking Xanax." At this I turned toward her and she continued hurriedly. "For that breathing issue I told you about. It's been helping, really it has. But then when I drink after I've taken one, it'll be all great for a while, and then suddenly I'll black out and not remember anything. That's what happened with that guy. You know, that short guy I told you about, with curly hair. At the Italian restaurant."

I remembered the guy, though I'd never met him, just heard about him as I'd stood in line with Erin at the pharmacy for Plan B. She said she'd found him unattractive, but that she was drunk and took him home anyway. The last thing she remembered was padding into her bathroom to get a condom. In the morning she'd looked at the used thing and panicked; it didn't look right. "I don't want to have this guy's baby," she'd told me. "In the future, everyone I sleep with, the guy has to be good looking, someone I can at least look at and say, okay, I could have his baby." She said she'd never get an abortion; she'd been raised Catholic. She'd looked somewhat excited when she said this, like a part of her wanted an accidental pregnancy to happen, which alarmed me. But as she swiped her credit card I supposed there was no reason Erin shouldn't have a kid if she wanted. She certainly made enough money to raise one by herself.

When I got home I felt unexpectedly exhausted, and lonely. I lay on my couch with my arm over my eyes and let my mouth turn down dejectedly. I thought about the guy I'd dated the summer before, how one afternoon he'd gotten barefoot and climbed the fig tree on my street, laughing as he dropped the fruit down to me. The weekend after that, apropos of nothing, he'd told me that he liked hanging out but didn't want anything serious, as if the intimacy of sharing fruit had suddenly made it all too much. There'd been a slight smile of satisfaction on his lips as he'd told me this, like he was enjoying exercising his upper hand. I'd told him goodbye and good luck. This shocked him; he said effetely that he hadn't meant he wanted to stop seeing me. I guess he'd really thought I was a pushover.

I wondered if maybe I was. In a vague sense, I knew why Erin was unhappy. But I felt powerless to help her. I did the same things.

Maybe I could change, with Christian. I thought about his saying he wouldn't see the other girls again, and this time felt kindlier toward his posturing. In a way we had a lot in common, shielding our insecurities with false bravado and toughness. He was arrogant, yes, but only because he was too terrified to look at himself more closely, to face the fact of his insignificance in the world. Weren't we all? I thought it was possible that we could protect each other, preserve each other's fantasies of self-importance.

I got up and went to my desk. The teenager next door was playing basketball on the driveway again. I typed to the beat of his dribbling and ended up working for hours, into the evening, dropping into bed early with a twangy headache that felt almost virtuous, like a sharp proof of productivity.

An hour later, I woke up when Christian called. There was a coddling solicitousness to his tone that assumed I would be feeling tender and vulnerable toward him, and in my groggy, curled-up state, I did. He asked me what my plans were for Christmas day. When I said I didn't really celebrate Christmas though I had nothing against it, he invited me to a potluck Christmas dinner he was having with a few of his friends. "You don't have to bring anything," he said. "Just show up."

"I can make something," I said. I wondered if Matt had warned him about my cooking for some reason. I thought I was passable in the kitchen.

"We could make something together," he said. "What do you like?"

At this I started making haphazard suggestions, but it became clear he'd already created a menu and bought the ingredients, which was just as well. We were to make turkey and sweet potato pie. He said there'd be six of us, and that he thought his friends would like me. He said this like a compliment without bringing up whether or not I might like them. This grated on me. I pictured myself as a demure and obedient child, being kept up after bedtime and trotted out to play an amateurish piano concerto for the dinner guests. At the same time I felt that child inside me grow eager and plaintive, looking forward to that impromptu concert, yearning to perform well. In my mind I petted the girl's head, trying to calm her anxieties. But I couldn't. She was hungry for attention, and strong-willed.

In the end I didn't end up helping much in the kitchen; Christian had almost everything done by the time I got there. He had me run the beater over the sweet potato mixture, then as soon as the pie was in, we started making out, somewhat theatrically, like we were acting out a scene in which we knew we'd be interrupted by the comedic sidekick. Still, we went at it for a while. He had my shirt wrenched up and me pinned hard against the fridge when the doorbell rang. We straightened up with an artificial sheepishness. His friend Jason arrived first via taxi with his law school girlfriend, Jenna. Then Amy, a girl Christian had met in an improv class a long time ago, came in with her acting class buddy, Jeff.

I disliked Amy instantly. A pretty, slightly bony brunette, she introduced herself to me in an ostentatious, overly-familiar way that somehow seemed to announce she'd met plenty of Christian's girlfriends before and had acted this way with each one. She and I sat flanking Christian, who took the head of the table, and she flirted with him occasionally, leaning over with her elbow on the table, her hand dangling over his thigh. Then she'd look over at me and wink, as if the flirting was some inside joke we shared.

She mostly focused on Jeff though, a dark, scruffy guy with nice arms. She had an obvious crush on him that got bolder with each glass of Pinot Noir. All of Christian's friends drank a lot, in fact, the empty bottles collecting on the table like spent exclamation marks. They apparently took the Christmas holiday seriously. By dessert they were lax and garrulous, playing with the food, spilling bits and drops, interrupting each other excitedly with banal platitudes about life. Christian was enjoying it. He'd let himself get quite drunk. His self-aware, self-revisionist tendencies were completely gone. Now he was shamelessly cheeky, wearing a loose, semi-permanent grin. This transformation gave me pause, though I was glad to see him looking free, liberated from the insecurities he worked so hard to mask. He started making silly double entendres and laughing hard at them. At dessert, he interrupted Amy and made an abrupt segway in the conversation to start discussing deadbeat dads.

"I'm not saying they shouldn't be held responsible, necessarily," he said, mirthful and loud. "But the thing is, they have no choice if you think about it, if a woman gets pregnant accidentally and she just decides to have the kid."

His eyes had a giddy, hooded look, like a mischievous boy trying hard to stay awake to see the results of a prank he'd set up.

"I totally support a woman's right to choose," he continued impishly. "Which is why, if she's made that choice herself, never mind what the guy wanted, shouldn't she kind of take on the consequences?"

The guests kept on their tipsy smiles but their brows tensed slightly, inclined to be agreeable but unsure how they'd suddenly ended up in this position. "I don't know if I'd go there, Christian," Jason said in a tone of mock caution, and the table laughed a little, good-natured and uneasy. I looked around with a nebulous discomfort. I was bothered that by virtue of being his date, I may appear to be agreeing with him if I stayed silent. Yet I didn't care to join in, not when Christian was so obviously fishing for attention, holding up his ridiculous bait with a desperate glee. And I didn't really want him to feel bad either. These were his friends, after all, and he'd invited me to meet them. It was Christmas. He was drunk enough to be oblivious to the tenor of the room. He grinned stupidly over his glass. I felt embarrassed watching him, but also wanted to be tolerant of his transparency, its needy innocence.

Jenna suddenly spoke up. "You know, my mom didn't ask for anything," she said, sounding petulant and defensive, but slurring girlishly too, "raising me and my brother alone. But she struggled. I don't know if she would have taken it, but it would have really helped if our dad had helped out, ever."

There was a short silence. Then Christian said, "Wow! I wasn't expecting that!" Everyone laughed. "Wow!" he said again, more chastened this time, but still laughing. "I take it back. Down with deadbeat dads. I can take it back, right?"

"Yes, yes, take it back," Amy said, waving her hand as if to dismiss him. She got up and clomped around the table in her heels, passing around the chocolate raspberry crumb bars she'd brought. She said they'd been a hit with her acting class. Then she inhaled dramatically, like she'd just remembered something. "Jeff's an ah-mazing actor!" Amy said. "We should do that scene from last week!" She tried to pull him up from his seat.

"Hey—It's relaxing time now," Jeff said, pointing at his wine and gently extricating his arm. He was on his second glass, like me; he was the designated driver.

"Oh, fine." Amy stalled for a moment, uncertain, then by herself started in doggedly on a short solo scene—an Ibsen monologue animated with big arm movements. I smiled at Jeff, rolling my eyes at Amy. He smiled too, shrugging. Then we clapped—Amy was taking her bows.

The night slowly devolved. Christian opened yet another bottle of wine despite protests, a Bordeaux he insisted everyone had to try. This finally started putting his friends over the edge. Amy drank a half glass, then got up to do another scene, pulling

Jeff by the arm again and begging "Please? Pretty please?" in a cringingly desperate way. Christian for his part started opinion-ating about Mel Gibson's latest DUI. By this time I'd learned to just quietly smile along, obliging him without responding to him, like his friends knew to do. When he realized no one was really listening, Christian gestured wider, until inevitably, he hit his wineglass. We watched it fall slow motion into the turkey carcass. "Well, there goes that," Jason said, then glanced over at Jenna, who had been sitting silent for a while. She looked like she was going to throw up. Jason took her out on the balcony for air, then popped his head back in. "I'm calling a cab," he said.

Jeff immediately suggested going too, but Amy was drunk and bratty, saying she was staying until Jason and Jenna left. The cab was going to be an hour. We waited in the dimly lit living room, Christian fiddling with iTunes and Amy yelling out requests then dancing jerkily by herself. Jason and Jenna came back in and clung to each other, swaying in a vague waltz. Christian took me by the waist and we twirled around a bit too. He'd lost his logorrhea; the dancing took all his concentration, and he was pretty good at it, better than I was. Seeing Amy watch us, I felt a small, peevish pleasure. Christian dipped me. I was afraid he was going to drop me, but he didn't, and this made me relax for the first time that night. His eyes looked darker now, hinting at a complexity that almost made his former drunken pontificating seem like a put-on.

When the song ended Amy had a change in attitude. She turned to Jeff and said, "Do you want to go?" She said this smiling with bedroom eyes, as if he'd just propositioned her.

When he said yes, she took his arm. I heard her heels clatter out through the apartment complex's courtyard.

The taxi came soon after that. As soon Jason and Jenna were out the door, Christian turned and grabbed me. I lost my balance and we fell on the floor. We rolled around, giggly at first, kicking our shoes off, then more sensually, then giggly again. We cycled back and forth; we couldn't stay serious enough to actually progress to a real sexual encounter, but it felt good all the same, playful and intimate. Then he propped himself up on an elbow and said, "I got you a Christmas present."

We went to the bedroom, where he fished a gift bag out of the closet. In it was a Malcolm Gladwell book from my Amazon wish list, and a silk eye mask. I'd told him I wore one when I slept at home. "For when you stay here," he said.

I thanked him sincerely. It was the most thoughtful gift I'd ever received from a guy, the most accepting. I leaned into him and we kissed deeply, and while we did, I remembered what he'd said about his tendency to jump into things too quickly. I didn't care. Maybe it would be different this time. It was happening fast, but without illusions. I already knew I could be embarrassed by him, and I was okay with it. It felt candid and clear-eyed, free from games.

"I got you a gift too," I said suddenly. I took his hand and led him outside in a half-run, the concrete icy against our bare feet. The night winds whipped around us powerfully. I opened the trunk and lifted out the scarf, the blue one I'd gotten for my sister. "It's like mine, but different," I said.

He turned it over in his hands, then wrapped it loosely around his neck and looked at me, as if for approval. "Thank you," he said. I shrugged happily. I felt resolute and proud, like I'd flouted some rule. "Thank you," he said again, then leaned over for a long press of his lips against mine. When he pulled away his face was in shadow and I couldn't read his expression, then he moved a little and I saw the glint of light on his teeth. I realized then he was still drunk, swaying, grinning blithely under the moon, content. I was disappointed realizing this, that he wasn't experiencing this moment as viscerally as I was. But I also felt a slight pull. He was happy, and he was with me, and I wanted to feel what he was feeling.

After the New Year, I went to Natalie's boutique again. I explained to Natalie why I needed another scarf and told her about Christian, which seemed to make her happy, like she'd been somehow instrumental in the romance. Then Natalie told me about her experience detaching from her mom.

"It was just a first step," she said. "But when she said we should go on a hike, and my brother said no, he just wanted to relax and watch TV, I agreed with him. In the past I would have just gone with my mom without question. I would have helped her try and guilt him too."

She sounded exultant.

"Then the next day, when I was packing up to leave, she asked me to stay until after dinner, and I said no, I wanted to beat the traffic. She didn't make a scene because my brother was there both times. I planned it that way to make it easier."

"Have you talked to her since?" I said.

"No. That's how I know she's mad." Natalie marched me over to the scarf section and presented the top one to me in a defiant gesture. Then she brightened. "So let me know how it works out with him," she said. "Maybe I'll start calling these the holiday love scarf."

That night I met Erin for drinks at Bodega Wine Bar. When I got there she was surrounded by a group of coworkers, most of who seemed to be her underlings. They looked at her with a glittery respect mixed with a certain impetuousness, like they were testing out being on equal footing with her, fellow drinkers at a bar. When I arrived they bought Erin a last drink and said their goodbyes. Afterwards Erin glowed, basking in the aftermath of their attention. She had the look of a valedictorian who'd finally received from school the attention she'd never gotten from her parents. I felt a swell of tenderness. We moved from the bar to a table that had opened up in a corner, then sat close to each other and made small talk in low tones, as if conspiring. I leaned my head on her shoulder for a moment in a show of feeling.

"I've wondered if I should be worried about you," I said.

"Worried? Why?" She asked in a flattered tone.

"The Xanax thing. I didn't realize it, that you were having such a hard time."

"Oh, that." She shrugged, then leaned over her glass of water and without lifting it, sucked from the straw. "I don't take them that much."

"I feel like maybe I made it hard for you to tell me," I said. "Like I was judgy about that short guy. It's just that it seemed like you were unhappy, so you were trying these random things, whatever came along, and they were making you unhappier." I paused, feeling genuine. "You deserve better."

She laughed mildly at this, like she was humoring a child. She put her arm around me and squeezed my shoulder. She felt strong and solid. "It's not like I suffered some sort of damage and I'm permanently tainted now. I just didn't like the guy, and I need to nix the alcohol and Xanax combo. Keep them separated. Church and state."

"Okay," I said. "You're right."

She was still smiling, more inwardly now, thinking. "Let's go for a walk," she said. "Actually, let's go to my place. I have a surprise."

Erin lived five blocks away. The streets were cold, but the air was still. I felt like we were inside a refrigerator, the traffic on Lincoln whirring steadily behind us. Once we started walking I noticed Erin's shoes, new gray pumps with rounded toes, then realized she was wearing a whole new outfit—a gray pencil skirt and a maroon silk shirt under her regular black coat. I complimented her and she stuck out her chest a little, gratified. She said it was her new look, part of a New Year's resolution. Her stride was brisk and her mood jubilant. She pointed out little details of her neighborhood's holiday decorations as we walked—the miniature tree in a shoe repair shop, the lone red ribbon around a ficus tree. As if on cue a green sedan glided by, the tune of "Feliz Navidad" floating out its windows. The car contained a nuclear family, elementary school–aged kids in the back seat; it came to a stop at the light in front of us. When it started moving again a homeless guy we hadn't noticed stood up from a doorway and yelled that Christmas was over. At this we turned the corner onto Erin's street.

As soon as I walked in the door I noticed the moving boxes. At first I thought she'd brought some extra stuff back from her parents' after the holidays, but then saw she'd taken her framed posters down. Erin grinned at my confusion. "Surprise!" she said. "I'm moving to New York."

"Since when?"

"I didn't tell you because I was afraid I'd jinx it. But the New York office had this senior manager position. My boss told me last week that I got the job, which was weird since we're on the same level now. They're paying for my move, and if I want, they'll pay for my MBA." Her eyes shone. "After that, I could really go anywhere."

I congratulated her, a bit uncertainly at first, then once I started to feel the logic of it, more heartedly. I'd miss her, but she was right. Moving would be good for her. It would rejigger the frayed puzzle pieces of her life, start to jolt them in place. She opened a bottle of champagne and even before we started drinking it, we started growing giddy and excited, imagining her future. I peppered her with logistical questions. She was going to leave in a week and a half. She started talking about renewal and clean slates, about how she'd get to start that relationship seminar there now. Her voice was somewhat tremulous, with a flustered joy.

"The fact is, it just hasn't worked out for me in LA," she said. "I've been living here a decade, and really, what do I have to show for it? There's nothing holding me here. I mean, friends, of course," she looked at me meaningfully, "but you know." She paused. "I didn't want to admit it because it seemed like admitting that I'd failed, but it doesn't have to be that way."

We nodded together in a fraught but accepting silence. We both surveyed the jumble of boxes.

"I've kind of started seeing someone," I said.

"Yeah, I know," Erin said, as if she'd been waiting for it. "Natalie told me."

Erin had gone in after work to exchange her scarf, to get a gray one that went with her new outfit. We must have just missed each other. Erin asked me genial, obligatory questions about Christian and seemed fairly happy for me. She poured us more champagne, then put on some music. "Pretty Young Thing" played, a cover by a woman with a feathery voice. I thought she filled the lyrics with fear and an ill-defined regret, bringing out the strange melancholy of youth and uncertainty in the lyrics. But the music only seemed to enliven Erin, who sang along at the chorus, keeping beat with her thumb against the glass. I thought about how nothing was fixed, that everything—songs, events—held only the meanings we affixed to them. I wondered if my mind had been perpetually stuck in one spot, dissolutely clinging to the uncertainty it was familiar with, adding that scrim to everything I saw. For a few seconds I saw myself as floating in a limpid, amniotic darkness that was comforting, but also keeping me in an ineffectual, fetal state.

Then the song ended, and Erin turned to toast the New Year again. We started walking between the boxes, Erin going over what she planned to take, what she wanted to sell. She gestured at the window and pointed at a big Christmas tree planted in a neighbor's back yard, its gigantic glass star gleaming from its high perch. The fog had come in and I couldn't see the real stars above it, but I could sense them up there, shining, patient.

You Are Realistic

The last time I saw Jeff on stage was in a dream, a dream of nostalgic contradictions, my private emotions unfurled and exposed by the stark presence of my body among other bodies, all twisting yearningly to stay in rhythm with the unstable logic of the dream.

In it, I was in Griffith Park for the Free Shakespeare Festival, alone on a square of blanket checkmated by all the other squares of blankets, hundreds of them, on which sat other women, also each alone, in varying postures of boredom. We were all waiting for the show to start. The stage undulated softly before us, and looking closely I saw its walls were a tangled façade of leotard-clad bodies, their small movements like an almost imperceptible dance. Jeff came on the stage looking young and impetuous, wearing his usual scruffy T-shirt and expensive jeans, the ones with the tricky zipper. A shiver ran through the crowd and I tensed with it, until the play was over in a flash, the wall disassembled into an excited mass of writhing bodies, and Jeff walked off the stage, toward me. He moved with a sharp tenacity, his cold, lithe body cutting like an ice pick through the summer air. His dark eyes glowered with a seductive danger. I stood up anxiously. But when he got close, he transmuted. I realized he wasn't actually Jeff at all but another guy, one with a sharp, deliberate haircut that looked almost peculiar against his blandly friendly expression. This guy was in his early twenties, a decade younger than Jeff and I, and he had an overeager jauntiness that affronted me. Our eyes met briefly, then still grinning, he walked past me, gleefully holding out his tin bucket for donations.

The next week I felt pulled toward Venice and went there, somehow convincing myself that it wasn't about Jeff, I just needed a change of scenery. I walked down Abbot Kinney aimlessly before settling on a coffee shop, one outfitted in minimalist warehouse style, glass and chrome and vaguely lab-like, the shelves lined with beakers and Chemex flasks.

Of course I found myself looking for Jeff there, though there was no reason why he'd come into this place. He didn't even drink coffee. Still, I took a seat and studied the crowd. The baristas were all rail thin, wearing skinny jeans and black vests over neat collared shirts, accentuated with bright bow ties. At the back of the café was a raised bar where customers sat facing forward, their row of laptops gleaming like polished teeth. From the stereo came music that sounded like The Supplies, but with heavier drums. A couple walked in wearing tennis whites, each holding an end of a baby blue surf board. They edged around the bar and disappeared through the swinging metal doors into the kitchen. I stayed distracted this way until close to closing time. It was only then, in the balmy dark illuminated by streetlights, that I finally wandered into Diane's Restaurant.

The restaurant wasn't crowded, but it took me a while to spot Jeff because he was on the other side of the bar, a customer. When I saw him, he was already studying me with an amused smile.

"You're here," he said.

He said he'd stopped by on a whim to see old friends; he'd quit bartending at Diane's months ago. I said I'd been in the area and just needed a quick drink. When he got off his stool and gave me a half-hug, his stubble grazed my skin, and the rest of my night as we talked, my cheek tingled and burned insistently.

I'd first met Jeff about a year before, at a Christmas dinner party thrown by Christian, my boyfriend at the time. Jeff had been dragged to the event by an acting buddy of his called Amy, who had an obvious crush on him. At the end of the night I'm pretty sure Jeff went home with her, though I never asked him about it.

A few weeks after that dinner, Amy invited Christian and me to her birthday party at Diane's. I didn't expect to see Jeff there until I spotted him mixing drinks behind the bar, looking put upon. Amy had obviously planned her party there so she'd have an excuse to see Jeff again, and realizing this, I felt a small tug of pity for her.

Amy had a brave game face on though. When she saw Christian she squealed and gave him, then me, a sloppy hug. She and her actor friends had taken over most of the restaurant's bar section, already a few drinks in and rowdy. I followed Christian to the bar. Jeff remembered us and said the first round was on him. "Thanks again for dinner," he said, looking at me. I told him Christian had done all the cooking. Jeff looked unconvinced but he said thanks again anyway; Christian responded by thanking Jeff for the wine. Then there was an awkward pause, and Jeff went to help other customers.

Christian and I stayed at the bar and drank somewhat lugubriously, watching the actors preen and pose with melodramatic, garrulous enthusiasm. Christian drank a lot faster than I did; he had a narcissistic but fragile sense of pride that he protected by drinking diligently. At the bottom of his glass Christian ordered another and got up, lubricated enough to join the fray. I told him to go ahead, I wanted to relax and finish my drink first. He hesitated for a moment but then gave me a wet, close-lipped kiss and left, his hand curled possessively around the new drink.

"Sorry about the noise," Jeff said, suddenly in front of me, drying a glass. He shrugged, smiling. "I think we're the only people here who aren't trying to get wasted."

I smiled back. At this he unexpectedly held my gaze. The gaze-holding came so suddenly that I wasn't able to look away, that instead I stared back at him transfixed, my senses slowly growing warm and nervy, confused. The moment felt visceral though it must have lasted only a few seconds, so that afterwards, when he made small talk with me in that genial, light tone of his, I was left with an incoherent, unmoored feeling that I tried to anchor by reminding myself that it really had happened. He was wearing the regulation dark jeans and black button-down of bartenders, sleeves rolled up, which on him looked sharp and precise, tailored to his lean form. He moved around fluidly, chitchatting with me between customers, the long row of stoppered wine bottles a glossy backdrop for his performance. There was a soft pop tune playing, its sound almost drowned out by the party, but audible in snippets if you listened hard for it, and it seemed only the two of us could hear that music, could sway surreptitiously to its secret rhythm. I wondered if Amy was watching us, if Christian was, but didn't turn around to look. We weren't doing anything suspicious. Jeff asked me how I spelled my name, and what neighborhood I lived in. I told him I lived in Santa Monica, and he said since I was so close I should come by once in a while. He said this in such a breezy tone that I really couldn't tell if he was coming on to me, or if he was just being nice, or if he got some sort of bonus for bringing more customers in. "I work Thursdays and Fridays," he said affably, then after a moment, added, "You can bring your friends too."

I asked him about the acting class, the one he'd been in with Amy, and he smiled like he was glad it was over. He poured another tray of shots for the actors; a Drew Carey type whisked it away. They seemed to be taking turns buying rounds, though Diane's was really a wine and specialty cocktail place. The party crowd had gotten considerably louder since I'd arrived, and the diners in the restaurant section kept fidgeting and looking over with a scowl, then turning their glares at Jeff, who'd shrug commiseratingly then go back to pouring drinks. Jeff said he'd just been cast in a play, *Antony and Cleopatra*, and when I expressed interest, said I could come to a rehearsal, at the Theatricum Botanicum in Topanga. That's when Christian came up, slinging an arm around me and setting his empty glass on the bar. "What's in Topanga?" Christian asked, tipsy and grinning. Jeff quickly told him about the play. "I'll let you know when the performances start," Jeff said, rather loudly, refilling Christian's glass. "I'll Facebook you guys."

"That would be great, man," Christian said. "We'll totally be there."

It was close to two in the morning when we left the bar, and on the way home to his place, Christian was drunk and affectionate and amorous. At a deserted stoplight he eased up my skirt and put his face between my legs, in a soft, almost drowsy way. I pressed my foot harder on the brake, as if in response. I closed my eyes. Then a car that had come up behind us honked, Christian sat up, and we moved forward.

Of course I never took any friends to Diane's. That was just one of Jeff's decoy phrases, let out there softly like a song past its prime to blend into the white noise of the crowd. He and I both listened hard for the tune though, and when it played, we moved to its pulse. A couple weeks later, I stopped by on a Thursday. I got there just before closing and took a seat at the bar with a glass of Viognier. Jeff's smile when he saw me seemed startled and expectant at once. We made light banter about good brunch spots and movies, delicately avoiding any mention of people we knew. We mimed an innocent friendship, though I felt his coworkers must have known what was going on, that my showing up there at all betrayed it somehow. Eventually, once we were out on the near-deserted street and walking, he grabbed my hand somewhat selfishly. He walked me to my car, which was parked on a side street under a sinister-looking tree, and in its murky shadow we made out, a crush of tongues and hands groping next to the quiet dumpsters. "Should we go somewhere?" he said. Then we parted and drove our separate cars to my place.

Once we were alone, he was shyer than I'd expected. He took my clothes off cautiously, as if any sudden movements might make me change my mind. "Is this okay?" he kept asking, and I think with anyone else this would have annoyed me, though with him it felt sweet. When he came he let his body collapse into mine and we lay cuddled that way for a long time, his face tender against my neck. I took shallow, heady breaths, because of his weight. Afterwards, side by side, we talked for a long time. We discussed unnecessarily personal subjects, about family and ambition, both of us answering questions in what seemed like obstinately direct ways, as if our situation demanded that we share these details. Despite that, our conversation still had the polite, back-and-forth manner of strangers who by sheer chance had been placed together at a wedding reception table. When I told him I was a freelance writer he said his father had recently self-published a book of poems, of which he was proud but his children not, the book being a compendium of their embarrassing childhood memories. The Kindle download was available for ninety-nine cents. Still, Jeff talked about his father fondly. I told him my only foray into acting was in the sixth grade, when I played Buttercup in the school production of *H.M.S. Pinafore*. I told him I was a lot better at the singing than the acting, at which point he started trying to get me to sing something from the musical. "Come on, just one line," he said, and when I refused he started tickling me, both of us laughing hard, until eventually we went at it again, more aggressively this time. After that, we lay in a near doze, tired but unable to fall asleep, taking turns starting brief, non-sequitur conversations. Right before we finally drifted off, Jeff made fun of his co-star, the Cleopatra of the play. "She hath such a celerity in dying," he said. "Like, seriously." We both laughed drowsily into our pillows, though I had no idea what he was talking about.

"Like a thin, vapid attitude," Christian said, when I asked him what celerity meant. I told him I was reading the play in preparation for the performance. Christian had gone to grad school for creative writing, though he'd dropped out after a year.

"It says 'swiftness of movement,'" I said, searching on Google.

"You're missing the nuance."

I nodded, though I didn't believe him. I'd never heard Christian just say the words, "I don't know." I thought I might ask Jeff about it later, give us something to talk about, though I wasn't sure when I'd see him again, or if I would. Even after it became a regular thing that winter, I wondered often what Jeff thought of me, though every time we met I was too afraid to ask. I supposed he liked that I wasn't an actress, that I could move to the beat of his tune without turning anything he said into a production. And maybe he liked that I had a boyfriend, that I couldn't push him for anything without seriously upsetting the fragile equilibrium of my life. It disconcerted me a bit, but I think he liked my easy predictability, that I evoked in him a feeling somewhat close to a pleasant boredom. By that I don't mean that the sex was bad. It wasn't, and that was a part of it too. And it was that memory I felt on my cheek, sitting at the bar with him a year later.

Our meeting was more awkward this time. The chairs forced us to sit facing forward, so that when I turned toward him, I was confronted with his distant, aquiline profile, his eyes slightly downturned and preoccupied. He was wearing a shirt I didn't recognize, with jeans that I did. I asked Jeff how the acting was going and he said it was fine, in what seemed like a slightly testy tone, but then he turned his head and asked about my work. I chattered aimlessly, nervous. The bartender, who seemed new, set down my glass of wine while glancing past me, then moved to the other end of the bar and glanced in the same direction again, at the last table still in the dining area. As I talked I turned and saw a popular singer sitting there, a girl I'd seen on billboards but couldn't name. She wasn't wearing any makeup and looked a bit shy, nodding softly while the people around her, all much older than her, jabbered urgently.

The place was otherwise empty. It was a Tuesday, close to midnight. The flat screen next to the bar was on mute, flashing through images of a man's mouth, eating an apple, licking a stamp, kissing a child. I stopped talking and Jeff and I both watched in silence, until we realized it was an advertisement for mouthwash. Then we looked at each other without comment, our lips sliding over our teeth self-consciously.

He spoke first. "Do you want to get out of here?"

Instantly his voice took me back to my old apartment, its close walls and flat, tatami-like carpet, the alcove of the bedroom area cozy and clandestine. I remembered that first morning after, when he got an audition call and slowly woke up as he answered it, talking in a confused then in a more excited way. I remembered how he looked, sleep in his eyes, fumbling around for his jeans where he kept post-its and a pencil. "Okay, I'll be there," he said, his voice groggy with morning. Then he got dressed without showering and after giving me a quick kiss, went straight to the audition. His hair looked good a little greasy, and I think he knew it.

Most of the time he'd just come to my place, but once in a while I met him at Diane's. I found out quickly he had his share of admirers there, the kind that kept ordering drinks to get his attention, until they got sloppy and shameless and sad to watch. The second time I went by alone, there was this one girl who had come dressed up in a blue-silk, babydoll-ish dress and hipster glasses. She sat at a small table with her friends and kept calling "Je-eff, Je-eff," and asking him to come over and settle one conjecture after another her friends had come up with about men and what they wanted. When Jeff went, they begged him teasingly for free drinks, and eventually, he obliged them. "They're regulars," he told me, shrugging.

He was the kind of person who ate in handfuls on the go, rarely sitting down for a real meal. At my place I'd make him peanut butter and jelly sandwiches or, if I was out of bread, feed him wasabi peas or trail mix, in those one-serving pouches from Trader Joe's. We'd sit in bed and eat with childlike pleasure, and I thought these little meals were more delicious in their simplicity, somehow more real and instinctual than Christian's elaborate dinner parties, with all their shucking of oysters and entertaining of strangers and cleaning up of messes.

I've made things with Jeff sound more idyllic than they really were. In reality it was mostly uncertainty and anxiety and confusion, if with an undercurrent of anticipation, since we never defined anything, never knew if this time might be the last time, that sense of trepidation growing more imminent the longer things went on. There were a few weeks when we saw each other quite a bit, but most weeks we didn't see each other at all, and we had a tacit agreement that we wouldn't comment on either of those circumstances. Sometimes, I felt closer to Christian and didn't return Jeff's texts, even when I was alone at home. Other times, Jeff ignored mine. Once I showed up at Diane's as planned and Jeff wasn't there. I was told he couldn't make it in that day by a female bartender who studied me appraisingly, after which I felt compelled to order and drink my requisite glass of wine anyway. Jeff texted while I was there to say he was sorry, rehearsal ran late, but later, trudging to my car alone, I found myself half-afraid and half-excited that I might run across him on the sidewalk, holding some other girl's hand.

We stepped out onto the balmy street. "Where do you want to go?" I said.

He shrugged. "What's open where we can actually hear each other?" His tone was casual, almost indifferent.

"Nothing," I said. "Not at this hour."

We looked around the streets as if willing something to open. Cars went by slowly, watchful at the crosswalks. A group of girls cycled by on their cruisers, laughing loudly, their skirts flapping against their thighs.

"I thought about you last week," I said.

"Yeah?" He turned and looked at me, his expression a friendly challenge. His hair moved probingly in the beach breeze, slowly, like it was floating in water.

"There was this actor that looked like you."

"A doppelgänger," he said, then smiled, though there was a tension in it, like this news spelled bad luck and pained him to hear. I wondered if this was one of those things you weren't supposed to say to actors, some sort of faux pas I didn't know about.

I looked down, feeling slightly dejected. I flashed through Jeff's different expressions, serious, sleepy, excited, indifferent, and now, this unhappy smile. At the end of those images I realized that my memories ran like an infomercial for something, though I didn't know for what, one of those ads that evoked only a mood, so at the end you were left with a vague sense of longing, though you didn't know if it fit, how long it would last, how long you'd be amused by the novelty of it.

"What about Mao's Kitchen?" I said. "They're open until three."

———————————

I went to Jeff's place only once. It was the night Christian and I had our first big fight. Christian's drunk expression had taken on a teeth-baring, aggressive cruelty, which was such a turnaround from his usual slack, garrulous state of inebriation that I didn't know how to react. In the end he'd apologized and we'd made up somewhat, but I also told him I needed time alone to think. Walking to my car, I felt a small thrill just from having had the gumption to leave Christian when he'd wanted me to stay, that I'd proved to him and myself that I was capable of a little agency. I wanted to extend the high. Driving, I called Jeff and asked him if I could come over. "Sure," Jeff said, in a bewildered tone, and gave me directions in a careful, halting manner. On the freeway, I felt an almost giddy state of freedom, tinged with fear. I tried not to dissect whether or not Jeff really wanted to see me. I sped, but as a precaution stayed behind a woman who was also speeding, in a blue Lexus convertible. She looked regal, her graceful arms extending benevolently toward the wheel, like a monarch performing a stately ritual. I mimicked her. I popped my sunroof. The night was cool and slippery and glittery with headlights, the 405 still busy after ten, the cars slowing to an enthusiastic cluster at the 101 then speeding up again in joyful little blurs. Once I got off the freeway at Van Nuys, I squinted for street signs, coasting past the brightly lit fast-food chains and the more dour-looking strip malls until I was plunged into a dark residential area and found the complex where Jeff lived—a boxy, functional multifamily housing unit painted a dirty shade of beige, its buzz-through gate staring toward the street with a mute, impassive expression. Walking up to it, I felt myself tense up, hesitant and vaguely regretful about having made myself an imposition. I took a slow elevator up to the third floor and when the doors opened, Jeff was there. I followed his taut shoulders through a complex maze of narrow hallways, until he held his door open and ushered me in.

Once we were inside Jeff seemed to relax somewhat. His apartment was a one-bedroom, small but so sparsely furnished it looked roomy with possibility. I moved toward him and we had sex on the cheap carpet in his living room, made enough noise that his neighbors in the apartment below him pounded against the ceiling. The sound was oddly wet, like a soggy mop, or damp socks. Afterwards we laughed, talking about movies with sex scenes we liked, playfully pushing and pulling at each other, our limbs lax and giving. Later, in bed, I said "We should do this more often." He squeezed my hand in response, cautiously.

In the morning at his coffee table, we ate kiddie cereal. The sugary crisps sang against my teeth. I apologized obliquely for inviting myself over, and he shook his head. "I had fun," he said, then added, "Now you know how we do it in the Valley." He looked up from his bowl, smiling impishly. He reached over me to get the remote, grazing my right breast, then for the next half hour we watched cartoons, him running his hands under my shirt in a lazy, intimate manner. Then I told him I had to go, I had a writing deadline.

He stayed on the couch with the cartoons on low volume while I combed out my hair in the bathroom. I yelled out to him that I'd read *Antony and Cleopatra*, and there was a short silence. "I admire her resilience," I said. "She's a really strong character, I think. Beyond owning Egypt and being a ruler and all that, she's powerful on a personal level. Like she just goes for what she wants, even full-on into suicide."

"She definitely creates her own drama," he said.

In the corner of his bathroom floor, I saw a pink elastic hair tie, dusty with disuse. I picked it up and shook it off, then pulled my hair back. If Jeff noticed, he didn't comment on it, just gave me that usual indulgent kiss when I said goodbye. But the rest of the day, whenever I felt my ponytail bob, I sensed a gnawing sort of anger grow in me, petulant and itchy to see things to their conclusion.

Mao's Kitchen was still doing a brisk business, the scrabble of late-night diners somehow looking glamorous and almost subversive in the dank, dimly lit atmosphere. We sat in the corner against the red brick wall. Chinese propaganda posters stared down at us with gaudy, self-sufficient pride. Next to us sat two blond European-looking girls with big teeth, sharing a gigantic plate of chow mein and talking in a guttural language I didn't recognize. A short busboy silently brought us a small bamboo bowl of wonton crisps, then came back with a red unguent for dipping. Jeff bit into a crisp, then chewed studiously, like he didn't exactly like the flavor but was still interested and accepting of it on an anthropological level. "I'm not that hungry," he said. "Do you want to split something?"

———

After the Valley visit, I didn't see Jeff for a while. Perhaps due to the chagrin from our fight, or fear that I'd call it quits, Christian grew more tender, obliging, and five months to the day after we'd started dating, asked me to move in with him. We sent out an invite to the housewarming to all our Facebook friends, which by this time included Jeff. "Congratulations," Jeff wrote on the event wall, "but I have dress rehearsal that night." To that Christian replied that we'd be there to see him in the play as promised, that we had even read the play, by we meaning me.

And go to see him we did. We drove up to Topanga opening night. Amy organized it—to "support" her friend Jeff—buying a dozen tickets and rounding up her acting buddies, plus Christian and me. But the outing was a bust. It was an unusually windy night, and the attendance at the outdoor amphitheater was sparse. The tickets Amy got were in the cheaper, upper tier, and sitting there, we could hardly hear a thing. At intermission

Christian argued with the usher to let us move down closer to the stage, without success. So for three hours we watched the actors bluster about the stage pointlessly, their floppy, Shakespearian costumes billowing comically. I paid special attention to Cleopatra's death, but the actress' portrayal of suicide was anything but swift. She died painfully slowly, writhing a little, in a manner that seemed realistic enough for a poisoning by little snakes. Afterwards we all clustered around Jeff, as if for warmth. Amy handed Jeff a bouquet. "Wow, flowers—Thanks," Jeff said, cradling the tulips in his arm awkwardly, like he'd been handed an unruly infant. Christian slapped Jeff's back. "That was a unique interpretation of Antony. So militaristic," he said. "Really fantastic." I agreed. When Jeff's eyes met mine we smiled at each other plastically, then looked away.

That first month living with Christian was a strange time. I remember some happy moments as we rearranged ourselves to accommodate each other's routines. I also remember things went bad quickly. That said, even in the badness there was a part of me that felt lucky. Christian's drinking got worse, but I was nursing my own imposter syndrome, and I think I believed to some extent that Christian's own self-loathing was what kept him from noticing my defects. I was proving to myself that I could eke out a relationship, could get someone to care about me enough to stay in it. And this gave me a sense of accomplishment high enough to blunt the lows. No one really seemed happy that spring anyway, not anyone I knew, not anyone who circulated through our little dinner parties, to toast endless nothings and fool ourselves into believing we were grabbing life by the handful. It's obvious, looking back now, that it couldn't last, but at the time I thought I was making things work, taking the butt-ends of life and molding something messy but tangible out of them.

———————————

We settled on Sichuan eggplant. A middle-aged Chinese woman wearing a Grateful Dead T-shirt took our order. "White rice or brown rice? Brown rice is fifty cents more," she said. We went with brown. When she left I asked Jeff what he did now that he was no longer at Diane's. He looked up sharply, then said he'd started a new job, as a broker at a small investment company. His expression as he said this was challenging, but also a bit run down, like he was returning to a battle he'd fought before. I expressed surprise and said congratulations. At this he softened a bit. His shoulders still had that self-protective edginess, but his brow relaxed and he suddenly looked older, more adult, like someone aware of his mortality. I saw he'd grown thinner, his cheeks hollowed out under the reddish lighting. I asked if brokers had a flexible schedule, like freelancers, and he shook his head a little impatiently.

"It just gets old, the struggling actor thing," he said. "I'm discovering there are things I want in life, maybe even more than acting."

I took this in. I tried to think of something encouraging to say that wouldn't come across as patronizing. "You always seem to land on your feet," I managed. For a second I thought he might turn contemptuous, but then he just smiled and said, "I hope you're right."

Every play has its metaphorical gun, each actor fiddling with it, hiding it, loading it with need and suspense and Eros, before inevitably, someone pulls the trigger. And fooled by Chekhov, I think that's how I thought life should be too, though I made a poor actor, and I wasn't in a play.

That's why I showed up on the closing night of *Antony and Cleopatra*. I was the one person sitting alone in the packed amphitheater, filled this time with older couples that looked like do-gooder types, committed to supporting their local community theater in retirement. I sat in the second row. That close up, Jeff looked like a parody of himself, his stage makeup garish and fierce. I remember the moment he spotted me, when he wasn't part of the main action and a little off to the side, scanning the crowd. He gave a very slight start when he saw me staring at him, before he resumed the scanning. After the play I waited around and went up to him. He was with a few of his fellow actors, who seemed to make him skittish. "You came back," he said in a loud, cheery tone, then gave me a jumpy hug. "You were great," I said, my hands still on his arms, then quickly let go and turned to his friends. "You were all great," I said. They murmured thank yous. For a moment, we were all silent, then Jeff said, "Come on, let me walk you to your car."

We moved away from the crowd, not touching. Once we were in the lot I turned to him and said, "I missed you." I leaned into him. He gently turned his head away and put his hands on my shoulders to hold me at arm's length. "Hey," he said. "I'm seeing Allison now." When I didn't respond he added, "Cleopatra," for clarification. I realized I must have already known this at some level, because while his words wounded me, the feeling they produced was one that I'd been expecting for some time, that I almost recognized. I welcomed it, embraced that small tingly sorrow. He was pushing me away, but there was a new tenderness in his voice and hands that made me think we were still connected. I shrugged like it didn't matter. "And?" I said.

He took his hands off my shoulders. "Come on," he said, his tone suddenly exasperated. "The show's over." He looked at me for a moment. "Look, thanks for coming. It was good to see you," he said. Then he gave me a little firm wave. He turned around and went back to the crowd, to his girlfriend. Watching him go, I thought for a second about making a scene, my own version of celerity in dying, wrecking whatever we had in one quick go. But I didn't. I didn't see the point. I thought about how tomorrow, the costumes would be returned and the stage drops dismantled, the performance turning into a nondescript line on the actors' résumés before, in a few years, disappearing altogether. I thought about how this little act between Jeff and me too, like any bad behavior, would now disappear into the anonymity of the city, the world going on like nothing ever happened.

Our food arrived. We unsheathed our chopsticks and started grappling with the slippery eggplant. "I've wanted to apologize," he said. "I feel like I wasn't very up front with you, when we were seeing each other, about what I wanted." As if on cue the European girls next to us started shifting about. One of them slipped a clean pair of chopsticks into her pink backpack. Then the girls wriggled through between the tables and were gone. Jeff started again. "I was sort of just trying to figure things out for myself, and I think you became the victim of that."

"Victim?" I said. I laughed testily. "I wouldn't say I was victimized."

"Maybe victim was the wrong word," he said quickly. "Anyway, I'm sorry."

"You don't need to apologize," I said. I looked at him rather hard, but seeing that his face had turned sincere, I felt my expression mollify too. "Actually," I said, "Christian and I broke up. Three weeks ago. It was a long time coming."

A quick look of dark, cynical pleasure flitted across his face before he recomposed his expression into one of empathy and gave me an understanding nod. Oddly, this reaction made me see him more tenderly. Sure, he was glad that things had gone badly for me, but it was still the first sign I'd seen that he'd cared, that my being with Christian had ever bothered him. I tried to picture how it would have been had Jeff and I actually made a go of it together, but I couldn't. We'd really been happier this way, using each other as a prop for one-upmanship, connecting only to show how focused we were in changing other, more important aspects of our lives. I shrugged to say I was over it, then nodded to the waitress for the check. He offered to pay, and when I let him, he counted out his bills in a careful manner that seemed both beleaguered and proud.

Fortune cookies in hand, we stepped outside. The fog was rolling in. The wet air hugged us as we walked, breathing in the musty scent of the sidewalk. The streets were still awake, quieter now, but trembling with energy. We passed the V-E-N-I-C-E sign strung up in lights, the homeless woman cocooned in her bright yellow blanket, the teenagers practicing skateboard tricks in the post office parking lot. When we got to the residential block we broke open our cookies. Mine said "You are realistic and others can relate to you." His said "Cherish home and family as a special treasure." After we read them aloud we nodded at each other, like the messages we got were about what we'd expected, and thus satisfying. I asked Jeff how things were going with Allison, and he started talking about her genially, how the production company where she'd been working at for years had just promoted her to a full-time position. I got the sense they'd moved in together, though he didn't say it explicitly. His teeth twinkled animatedly under the streetlights. He asked me where I was living now and I told him I was back in Santa Monica. Saying this, I realized I felt happy, thinking about my little apartment with its new hardwood floors and its tiny parking spot. It seemed untainted—a place perfectly arranged to fit, clean and exact and waiting for my return.

We got to the corner of Abbot Kinney and stopped there, unsure what to do. Jeff offered to walk me to my car and I said that was okay, I was only a block away. Before he could hug me I stuck out a hand, with mock seriousness, and we shook hands firmly, mirth in our eyes. "Good luck," he said. "With everything." I wished him the same. Then we let go, I gave him a little wave, and we went our separate ways, he to his car, I to mine.

Sutures

I was at a competition of sorts that Friday morning, something of a cross between a beauty pageant and a modeling contest put on by upstart organic fashion companies. More than three hundred girls had ponied up the $20 application fee for a chance to be crowned "Spokeswoman for the Environment," a title that came with $2,000, a shopping spree, and a fashion spread in a just-launched nature magazine. The twelve finalists had been selected and brought to an airy home decor store in West Hollywood that had been cleared out for the occasion. That's where I sat now with a notebook and camera on a white fold-up chair, waiting for the show to begin.

I sat in a jaded agitation, not because of the show but because of what had happened before it, with Alek. I'd been seeing him for a few months and we were in that weird space where we had a fair sense of each other's messy characters but still tiptoed around on good behavior for the time being. Alek was an affectionate guy I loved being alone with, but there was a rambunctious side to him that unnerved me in public, when he sang along to background music or interrupted strangers' conversations, though people seemed to like him, responding in kind. He whistled loudly whenever he came across something he liked. I assumed this exuberance was a cultural thing, he'd immigrated to the US ten years ago when he was twenty-five, though I couldn't say for sure because I didn't really know any other Russians. He was in AA. He said he'd made a lot of money in finance but lost it all partying before going into rehab, which stuck the second time around. Now he owned his own small company, offering financial restructuring advice to struggling businesses. He seemed sincere in his quest to become a better person, to take life at face value, though I got the sense that he didn't quite take me seriously. I was a freelance writer, and at the time I was covering a lot of kitschy events, restaurant openings and local festivals and the like, where the big attractions were the B- and C-list celebrities that showed up to promote one product or another. Though we were the same age, when I talked about my work, Alek listened carefully but with an expression that to me seemed somewhat paternal, like my work was a cute little hobby that he nevertheless needed to be encouraging about. It was that expression he'd given me over coffee and toast at my place that morning, and I continued to grouse over it at the event as I fiddled with the settings on my point-and-shoot.

I started to feel better though, as the start time neared. I was sitting in the front row, on a chair that literally had my name on it along with that of the magazine. PR girls milled about, jittery and eager to please, offering press kits and cucumber water. I sipped from a clear plastic cup feeling official, legitimate. I thought if Alek came with me to one of these, he might see me differently.

The event began. It was like a runway show with hiccups, the girls strutting out in trios to techno and posing in a row at the front, at which point the music would cut unceremoniously and each girl would drone on about the environmental aspects of the clothes and designers. The girls looked skittish standing there, most of them not professional models, one blond's chin actually quivering desperately. Still, there was a certain dramatic insouciance to the whole thing. Lights popped. Digital cameras whirred through their gratuitous shutter noises. The writers held their voice recorders aloft, wrists cocked, or scribbled furiously, though none of us needed the notes; it was all in the press kits.

The finalist I planned to focus my article on was in the last trio. She was a twenty-six-year-old called Lana. I'd picked her because, according to the bios, Lana was a vegan and thus a good fit for the vegetarian magazine for which I was covering the event. Lana had even turned her husband vegan, when they'd married two years before. My editor said that if Lana won, it would be a triumphant feature profile, if not, a heartwarming underdog story. It was only when I googled Lana, clicking through to the fifth or sixth page, that I'd found out she wasn't new to being in front of the camera, that she'd posed for a good amount of soft-core pornography before getting married. The photos still online seemed tastefully done, erotically lit with carefully draped hair and sheets. Lana had taken her husband's name when she'd married but otherwise didn't seem

to have made much of an effort to change or hide her past identity, a choice about which I felt a nebulous respect. I wondered
if I should mention the porn to my editor, or if doing so would
just be spreading idle gossip. This wasn't the Miss America pageant, after all. I wondered if the photos were how she'd met her
husband, an older real estate guy who seemed moneyed. Since
the wedding Lana volunteered for Farm Sanctuary and gave the
occasional fermenting workshop at a local raw restaurant. In the
press kit photos she looked like a fresh Audrey Hepburn type.

And Lana did have some of that poise in person too now,
walking down the makeshift runway, though her posture was
less precise, more inviting in a lax, giving sort of way. She made
an impression, moving with a formulaic sashay in a blue dress.
The cut was demure but the fabric slippery, the silk shivering on
her skin. When she spoke, instead of reciting the product info
in the press kits like the other girls, Lana said she was especially
proud that the brand she was wearing made use of reclaimed
materials and that all clothes should be (considering the detri-
mental environmental effects of making new clothing), organic
or not. The fashion industry's disposable attitude toward clothes
led to a whole host of unseen travesties—child labor, sweatshop
conditions, chemical leaching, water pollution, landfill waste—
problems, she said, even many so-called green companies happily
turned a blind eye to. "Of course," she said, laughing indulgently,
"I'm not talking about any of the companies here. These companies are making fashions that last, the kind you'll want to pass
down to your grandchildren, the very opposite of disposable!"
The crowd seemed to be with her, nodding along. "Some of you

might remember that old PETA campaign, 'I'd rather go naked than wear fur,'" Lana went on. "Well, I say we start a new campaign. I'd rather go naked than wear new!"

There was agreeable applause. For a second I thought Lana was going to take off her dress; her left hand had started fiddling with a strap during the speech. But she didn't. She put both hands on the mic and went on. "We've heard the mantra—reduce, reuse, recycle. But in my opinion, we could just reduce that saying down to reuse. When we reuse, we *are* reducing what we need. We *are* recycling what we have." At this the emcee made a small wrap it up motion and Lana nodded at him energetically. "Okay, they're telling me my time is up, but as you can see, I'm passionate about these issues!" She made a fist, and shook it jokily.

The crowd laughed and applauded again. I clapped along, skeptical, but interested in spite of myself. Lana stepped back and the last two girls gave their spiel, but no one was really paying attention anymore. After Lana's performance, these girls' recitations of press kit fodder sounded especially canned and false, boring, and even worse, status quo. The audience, mostly writers on the environmental beat, had grown restless, discomfited by the tainted histories of their own clothing but also empowered to do better, as if a new focus on recycled fashion would suddenly turn them sexy and articulate and charismatic too.

The emcee took the mic and stammered out a few ingratiating sentences about the fashion sponsors without whom which this event would not have been possible. Then more confidently, he introduced the next competition: swimsuits. "In the spirit of reuse," he said, "the finalists are wearing what they already had in their wardrobes. None of these swimsuits are new!"

I thought it more likely that the competition hadn't been able to find a swimsuit sponsor, but the announcement nonetheless had an exciting effect. The two cameramen shuffled closer. This time, all twelve girls came out in a long row. Most of the girls were in demure suits, the kind their mothers would have approved of, but Lana had on a skimpy red thing, with a bottom that looked close to, but wasn't quite, a G-string. Her bikini top was more substantial, with solid cups and padding. Even more than the near nudity, Lana's self-assurance stuck out like a bold, throbbing thumb, her simple contrapposto stance almost lascivious compared to the somewhat embarrassed, apologetic postures of the other girls. To her credit, Lana's bikini looked like it could have been hand-crafted, something that had been fashioned out of a bigger, less stylish suit.

The cameramen ran back and forth, panning for angles. The crowd, largely women, clapped obligingly, with a mix of admiration and jealousy and, perhaps, muted annoyance. In fact, at that moment, I felt rather annoyed myself.

I didn't consider myself to be an environmentalist, though an online search of my name told a different story, thanks to all the hippie articles I'd written for the vegetarian magazine over the years. Those bylines had certainly fooled Alek. On our third date, he'd brought me a bouquet of lilies, gleefully pointing out the VeriFlora certification label, his way of letting me know he cared about me, enough to google my name and act on what came up, in any case. I didn't have the heart to tell him the certification didn't matter to me; I knew exactly how much the leftie lilies had cost him, having written the article promoting them, after all. It's not that I didn't care at all about the environment— I'd watched *An Inconvenient Truth* and bought organic oranges at Trader Joe's and separated my recyclables—but I felt the idea of environmentalism was something that circulated far outside and beyond me. I sensed that becoming an environmentalist would mean entering a sort of miasmic, otherworldly society, one that would require exploration with a Margaret Mead–like tenacity I had neither the interest nor time to develop.

Environmentalists seemed an angry, combative lot anyway, quick to point fingers with holier-than-thou attitudes while splintering into smaller and smaller factions in the manner of religious denominations. There were the older moneyed hippie types, with their gaggle of kids in charter schools and heirloom tomatoes in raised gardens. Then there were the younger ones, with their hipster glasses and punny blogs and titillating T-shirt slogans, like "Go Green: Fuck a Vegetarian!" Those kids put-tered around documenting their "activism" for Tumblr accounts with their camera phones, proselytizing for the environment with a fervent yet deadpan kind of sincerity I had a hard time distinguishing from irony. It was those young bloggers that seemed to be having a good time at this contest now, tweet-ing out their picks while tittering Perez Hilton–style about the cellulite on one of the girls' thighs before going on to say, "But she looked good in that dress. Natural. Thick," then nodding at each other seriously. To them environmentalism seemed re-duced down to sound bites and photo poses. And maybe in a way

I was jealous of them, of Lana too, her youth and enthusiasm, of how effortlessly she went off script to make what she had to say sound important and urgent. Maybe this is what environmentalism needed, a pretty face, bikini waxes, one-word mantras. I imagined Lana at the award party to take place that night, being crowned the winner in her heels, giving a speech about changing identities and changing worlds, about being flexible enough to use whatever we had to save the planet. The speech would be motivating in its own nakedly optimistic way, as if any problem could be resolved, or at least made beautiful, if we just stripped down to work it. Sure, it was exactly the kind of thing that made Alek take my work unseriously, but I also thought if he were here, he would listen to her, let himself be drawn in.

Which I suppose explains why I felt annoyed. Lana's call for change was infectious, yet what she was advocating as a solution—rehemming clothes to make them smaller, basically—seemed obscenely frivolous in light of the gravity of the problems for which she was to stand in as a spokesperson. It was hard to picture how Lana would actually advocate for serious change, like instituting a carbon cap or convincing people to relocate away from the New Jersey shoreline. Then again, maybe she could. Though there was an obvious, attention-mongering side to Lana's personality, her act as a whole had been on message, inviting, her tone sincere and positive. People wanted to give her attention. Maybe she could in fact convince stalwart Jerseyans to relocate. I pictured her in her bikini at the beach, strutting inland at the head of a long line of families, who pedaled along behind her, sweating industriously as they pulled their kids and belongings in refurbished bicycle trailers. I imagined someone taking a photo of this exodus, then posting the photo on Facebook, where it collected likes. Lana certainly had a can-do attitude. If nothing else, her reused clothing solution was tangible, doable. She even knew how to make it look good. I kept letting my mind circle around this way until I grew exasperated with myself for thinking so much about it. I wasn't selecting the head of the Environmental Protection Agency here. I was at a beauty pageant, for Christ's sake.

After the lilies, I'd tried googling Alek too, but wasn't able to find out much of anything about him. His full name sounded pretty unique to me, but apparently it was like John Smith among Russians, and unbeknownst to me until then, there was a gigantic Russian population in Los Angeles. Alek also just didn't have the kind of job that put an online identity out there. Discovering this, I felt at a disadvantage. My articles revealed a lot about me—places I'd visited, people I'd interviewed and liked, my relative worth in the freelance writing market, and even my bra size, wedged into a pseudo-personal article I'd written on the difficulty of finding cute, organic underwear. On top of that, the writing painted a skewed picture of me. The upbeat, gregarious tone I was hired to pen presented me as a sort of urban Pollyanna, someone in the know yet still unabashedly optimistic, almost chirpy. Thinking about the sincerity of my online persona made me wince, yet I really didn't see any easy way of correcting this image. In contrast, Alek remained a blank slate. I could learn nothing about him except what he chose to tell me about himself, and I resented this, though he kept telling me he was an open book. "Ask me," he'd say, facing me with this calm, patient expression, something I imagined he picked up from AA and its insistence on honesty. But I was reluctant to ask. I did find out a few things—he'd been married, he and his ex-wife had separated eight months ago, and he still paid the lease on the condo where she lived—but beyond that, any question I could think up seemed to reveal too much about my own vulnerabilities. I assumed he wasn't quite divorced yet, but didn't press to find out if he'd filed the papers. I felt asking about that would be like exacting some reassurance that he pictured something long-term with me, when in reality I was ambivalent myself. So I just kept grousing about it, not asking.

The chairs were whisked away and trays of champagne and mimosas brought around. The girls, back in the dresses from the beginning of the show, mingled with the now standing crowd. Lana was clearly a media favorite. She stood giving informal interviews close to the front, the better to pose for photos against the vinyl backdrop. The sponsors, most of them judges for the competition, watched as the journalists circled her, waiting their turn. There were a few judges outside the fashion industry too, including a short man with sad eyes who headed up the local Surfrider Foundation chapter, and a raw vegan cookbook author, a half-Japanese, half-German woman who was in her early forties but looked to be in her late twenties. I'd interviewed her a few months before for the vegetarian magazine's "Ask a Chef" feature. She too was watching Lana, through the corners of her eyes. I guess I was watching Lana also, the way she leaned into her interviewers as she talked, asking their names, her expression engaged and welcoming, vaguely presidential.

Soon she'll be channeling a magnanimous queen receiving her subjects, I thought. Still, I had to talk to her. It was already decided that she would be my story. As the crowd ebbed I edged up and waited for a tall, balding man to wrap it up. He talked to Lana while pumping her hand urgently, not having let go after the handshake. She squeezed back, her eyes in a friendly crinkle. "I actually made that bikini myself," she said. "From my mother's old suit."

"Wow," the man said. "Just, wow. You really practice what you preach."

He didn't seem ready to step aside anytime soon, so I piped up. "What you said about reuse," I said. "It seems to have really struck a nerve."

"I hope so," she said brightly. She managed to extricate her hand and extended it to me. I introduced myself and the magazine, and when I did, she took in a sharp, excited breath. "I love you guys!" she gushed. "Honestly, you guys are the one magazine that I feel—gets it." She looked at me meaningfully. At this the balding man slunk away reluctantly. I felt a strange mix of pride and embarrassment, like I'd gotten away with some small lie of omission. I noticed that up close, her face was a bit drawn, with a tightness to the jaw.

I thanked her. "You're obviously a gifted fashion designer yourself," I said. "What advice do you have for women who, say, can't sew?"

"Oh, but they should learn!" she said. "The sewing machine—it should really be considered one of our major environmental tools. For women, especially. Our grandmothers had the right idea, don't you think? They were so self-sufficient, making exactly what they needed for the family in the sewing room. The kitchen too!"

I wanted to shoot back about this domestic women thing, but demurred. "We're planning to do a feature. Maybe we could chat at the party?"

"Absolutely," she said. "Could I get a card? I have so much to talk to you about."

I handed her one somewhat reluctantly. When I turned to walk away I nearly collided with a passing tray of mimosas, and took a flute, as if in apology. Sipping against a wall, I decided that it was probably a good thing, after all, that Alek wasn't here, even though I was still vaguely curious about how he might respond to Lana, if his interest would be as blatant as the balding man's had been. Lana really had something that made men stand at attention. I remembered a conversation Alek and I had had, when we shared what we thought each other's strengths and weaknesses were. The talk was an assigned exercise for some leadership course Alek was taking at the Landmark Forum, another one of his quests for self-improvement. I couldn't really remember what he'd said my strengths were, but I recalled that when we got to the weaknesses part, he'd said that I had a trudging sort of attitude. At least that's how I interpreted his words. The actual phrase he used was "opposite of full of life," which depressed me then, to the point that for a few days, I really did go around feeling pretty lethargic. Later he said that wasn't what he'd meant, that it was a language issue, and that the word opposite was too extreme, he'd just meant something less than totally full of life, and that perhaps that was a good thing, he liked that I had both feet on the ground. His explanation hadn't made me feel much better, though the phrase "opposite of full of life" became a kind of joke between us later on. Thinking about it now, I wondered if what Alek had wanted, what he had expected after googling my articles, was something more like Lana.

Irritated, I eavesdropped uninterestedly on the raw vegan author making small talk with a fashion designer. The author seemed to be jockeying for free clothes to wear during her book tour. "I only wear companies I feel proud to represent," she said, "to spread the word, to other people." I missed the next few words, but then heard her say "environmentalism with legs."

Sure, legs. Of course. I thought back to my interview with this cookbook author, conducted over a ridiculously early dinner at Lukshon, when the restaurant was otherwise empty. She'd taken me into her confidence immediately—I seemed to have this effect on interviewees—and confessed she was neither raw nor vegan. She had been for seven years, but eventually she'd gotten sick and started eating first cooked food then meat, having been told to do so by an acupuncturist, then a holistic Chinese health practitioner, then a medical doctor she finally consulted when her hair started to fall out. She looked surreptitiously around the restaurant before ordering the crispy whole fish. She said she generally didn't eat animal products in public, because she didn't want her fans to catch her on camera doing so. It would be bad for book sales. She said people thought a raw vegan diet made her look the way she did, but that really it was genetics, and that she counted calories and did a crazy amount of P90X. Of course, all this was off the record. Later that night, after she emailed a recipe from her book to feature with the interview, I checked her Twitter feed to read this: "Why do people want fake vegan leather to look like real animal leather? I want my fake leather to look really fake!" It had gotten fifty-three retweets, mostly from followers with handles like @goveganordie. Seeing this made me snort derisively, but I wasn't actually that put off by her duplicity. I wrote for a vegetarian magazine, after all, and wasn't a vegetarian. What I felt for her was mostly a distant, confused kind of pity, the sort I have for drug addicts, or world hunger. I saw her writhing desperately to force in a divider between her public image and private life, all for the sake of a few thousand Twitter followers. Her actual lived world seemed small, with just a Vitamix and a matching set of dumbbells. She said she hadn't had a serious boyfriend in a long time, and I could see why, she had a rather pinched, aggressive personality that seemed to be standing guard over a sodden childhood wound. The whole raw vegan thing was part of this, something that gave her a concrete, exterior identity despite her private flouting of its rules. She seemed, in short, to be incapable of bridging the vast gap between her two selves, and resigned to living in the caustic gap between them, always looking over her shoulder.

It was this gap that seemed to be missing from Lana's life. Her insouciance, her devil-may-care attitude, confetti-ing nude photos of herself all over the internet, then marrying a rich guy and flitting about preaching reduce. No, reuse. I imagined Lana at her sewing machine darting her G-string, trying it on, then darting it a little smaller and trying it on again, this time taking photos of herself in front of the mirror and tweeting them.

The cookbook author exchanged cards with the fashion designer in parting, then spotted me. She walked over and stood next to me in a familiar, collusive way, our arms touching, like we were close friends about to continue a private conversation we'd started long ago. She said she really didn't have time for this, she needed to be getting ready for her book tour, which started next week. I ask her who her pick was.

"The token Asian," she said, and laughed tetchily.

"I don't know," I said in a lilting, facetious tone. "She's one of five blonds."

She laughed again, this time with a disgruntled shrug. She sipped her cucumber water.

"You should have entered this yourself," I said. "You would've won."

She flicked her wrist dismissively. "It's not the kind of exposure I want," she said. "It's desperate."

I nodded, mulling this over. "I think she'll win," I said, pointing my chin at Lana.

The cookbook author sniffed. "She's so obvious. But you're probably right." She seemed to realize something, and straightened up. "This isn't like an interview right now, is it? Do you want a quote or something, for your article?"

At that moment the event photographer came and stood in front of us. Without prompting we turned a little sideways, put arms around each other, and smiled. The camera clicked three times.

A few years before, I'd been a judge myself. It was for a cooking contest, organized by the vegetarian magazine, which had flown into LA three readers whose submitted recipes had garnered the most votes on Facebook. The weekend was an unusually busy one for the magazine—three of the editors were in New York for Natural Products Expo East—which is why they'd made me judge, suddenly slapping me with the title of contributing editor to make it all seem less ad hoc. That's how I found myself in the magazine offices in El Segundo one day, officiating behind a cheap, veneer wood cubicle desk, trying to chew in a knowledgeable and impartial manner under the anxious gaze of the three finalists, two from the Midwest, one from Texas.

The most unexpected part of the ordeal was that the Texan, called Bryanna, was a very tall and obvious cross-dresser or transgender. I didn't ask which. She'd shown up in a bright red dress, a high-necked thing overlaid with lace. Her sizeable shoulder muscles strained the sleeves taut, and her mannerisms were rough around the edges. Seated face to face, I congratulated Bryanna on making it this far, and she said liltingly, "I knew I'd make it in Hollywood one day." Then she added, "Or at least in El Segundo," and guffawed, slapping the table.

Bryanna laughed and talked a lot, in a cloying, overly familiar way, eager to pretend she could be one of the girls. "That's what she said," she kept saying, turning anything she could into a teenage innuendo, and each time I and the other two finalists, all more stereotypically female, laughed politely. I think Bryanna's attitude was intended to make it seem like she didn't notice or care about the discomfort around her, but we all became hyper-aware of her growing anxiety. The tension reached a peak when it came time to make the videos, short clips of the finalists that the magazine wanted to post online.

"Sit pretty," the cameraman, a gay Filipino guy called JD, kept saying to Bryanna. "Nice and pretty."

"Like this?" she said, flicking her hair. She turned her face to the left. "This way?"

"No, don't move around," JD said. "Sit pretty."

"This *is* my pretty side," she said, with a testy laugh this time.

What JD was trying to get Bryanna to do was pull her knees together. Her muscular white thighs were splayed apart mannishly and we could see halfway up her skirt. But no one wanted to actually say this, so we all just watched Bryanna try on different facial expressions. In the end JD zoomed in closer, to capture just her head.

"That's perfect," he said after the first take, and took down the tripod.

Bryanna looked confused; the other finalists had gone through a half dozen takes each. I thought she might protest. When she looked at me I smiled at her and nodded encouragingly. "You're a natural," I said. This seemed to placate her somewhat. After the finalists left, I watched the footage with JD. "You could have at least warned me she was going to be a six-foot-three tranny," he said, elbowing me. I shrugged, laughing, though I felt irritated. I'd wanted to tell Bryanna that she didn't have to try so hard, but I hadn't known how to do so without making her feel even more self-conscious.

And maybe it wouldn't have helped anyway, maybe it would have been worse if Bryanna had been more relaxed. Maybe this was about as good as things could go for her, for all the contestants. The whole deal seemed ill-planned and unprofessional to me, and I felt bad for these three readers who'd taken the contest so seriously, fretting about presentation and plates getting cold, stammering a little as they explained to me what they were trying to "do" with their dish. Their servile, ingratiating attitudes toward me had made me cringe inwardly, ashamed for them, and for me too. I really knew nothing about food.

Of course, Bryanna's video was never posted. My editor picked one of the Midwesterners as the winner and, diplomatically, posted only her clip and photos. If Bryanna was unhappy about that, I never heard about it. For a few weeks I wondered about her. I wanted to understand her motivations. Unlike the Midwestern women who'd practically blended into the background, Bryanna had wanted badly to stick out, to be noticed, with her red dress and gigantic heels. Yet she must have known the kind of attention she'd receive would be the awkward, avoidant kind. Was that attention to her still better than none? Or did she imagine that this time, on her big trip to Los Angeles, she'd wear a red dress and somehow the world would see her differently, react to her the way it did to women like Lana?

That night, at the closing party held at a new dance club in Hollywood, short videos of each of the finalists were shown to showcase their "environmental journeys." The two hundred or so partygoers, mostly twenty-something blogger types in skinny jeans, stood impatiently on the dance floor with drinks in hand and heads cocked up, watching the projection on the white wall. The video footage itself looked amateurish, shot at home by the girls themselves, but the clips had been montaged together by a professional editor to give real drama and pathos to each girl's life. Watching them, I slowly came to think that perhaps I'd judged these girls too quickly and harshly. Sure, some of the pretty ones looked like they'd done only token beach cleanups. But others, including Lana, who through her video I discovered was Russian too, had really been chosen for their environmental activism. Lana's video told a typical immigration tale but with a twist; her parents had come to the US and settled not in a city to work, but in a really rural part of Montana to be hippies. Her father, now dead, had had some liver and kidney disease, probably due to polluted water he'd grown up drinking, and to combat it, the family grew and ate their own organic food. At this point

Lana's story bifurcated, on the one hand telling an idyllic tale of swimming naked and climbing trees, on the other describing a crushing poverty and hinting cryptically at some sort of murky familial abuse. At school she faced bullying and racism; she responded in her teenage years by cutting herself and growing a Mohawk. "I was so angry," Lana said in the video, her eyes welling up. It wasn't entirely clear how, but environmentalism had given her a productive way out of her anger.

I wondered if the porn had also helped in some way. There was little in Lana's story that reflected my own, but I felt an instinctual connection to her nonetheless. Others felt it too. She had revealed through the video a poignant kind of personal suffering that showed that what she'd gone through was unique, yet open and accepting of all of us, so that we could gaze at that suffering, touch it, involve ourselves in it. Of course the masochism to all this confessionalism was somewhat disturbing too, but we still all wanted to revel in it—the edited, sanitized version of it anyway, the once-festering, pulsing wound now disinfected but left unbandaged so we could run our fingers over the skin, clean and ruddy and swollen around the neat sutures.

Afterwards, the party really began, with disco lights and a DJ playing house. I stood near the bar, watching people gyrate on the dance floor. I started picking out the finalists in this mass; they were spread out almost perfectly evenly through the crowd, each one ensconced in her own little pulsating orb of humanity.

It was a little after eleven. I thought about leaving, Alek would be just getting out of his AA meeting, but the winner hadn't been announced yet. I noticed the judges clustered together in a corner, deliberating.

Suddenly Lana was beside me. She gave me a loose, exuberant hug. She looked like she'd already had a few drinks, her face a wet grin and her eyes loose in their sockets, very different from the sincere, tremulous look that had been captured on film. Still, her enthusiasm was infectious. We yelled at each other over the music. I told her I liked her video. She nodded back energetically; I could tell she hadn't heard me right.

"I totally didn't think I'd make it this far," she said, spitting a little. She started talking about the other girls, how they'd all been speculating about the judging process and where each of them stood. As she talked I watched her loose, happy face and wondered what secret it was she was keeping about her family. Her tipsy attitude now reminded me a bit of a girl that had lived on my floor freshman year in college, the one that had broken her hip when a guy she was having drunken sex with in a fraternity bathroom dropped her on the floor. I hadn't been there, but apparently everyone else had been, had watched her get wheeled out by the paramedics with her pants down. She'd been in too much pain to care at the time, but afterwards, she'd dropped out of college.

If this type of thing happened now, there would be photos and videos documenting the incident, circulating among the kids' digital devices to be gawked at, zoomed into, photoshopped. Suddenly I felt an overwhelming gratitude that I'd grown up in the days before cell phones and Facebook. At least then the past really could be glossed over, almost forgotten with the help of new friends and a new hometown. Now, even big cities afforded no anonymity; anyone could do a reverse image search.

Not that I was against technology. On one of our earlier dates, neither Alek nor I could remember where we'd parked in the gigantic Santa Monica Place structure. Luckily the mall had just installed cameras, one pointed at the rear of every parked car. These cameras were linked up to little kiosks that let you locate your car by typing in the license plate. When Alek typed his in, the machine told us the floor and quadrant, and shot us back a real-time video of his car, waiting quietly in its spot. "This is perfect!" Alek said. "Every parking lot should have this." When we got to his car he said, "Wave for the camera!" And we did. His easy exuberance rubbed off on me when I was with him. Later that night, cuddled on my bed, we pretended to watch *Breaking Bad* on my laptop for a while before starting to fool around. When he went down on me I closed the laptop—the dialogue was distracting—but after I came and we took the rest of our clothes off, he repositioned the laptop and asked, "Can I open this?" He said he wanted to see me. The blue light of the welcome screen glowed against our skin in a way that made the experience feel like a performance, and we moved against each other in a desiring yet somewhat ritualistic, programmatic fashion. Oddly, afterwards, I felt a lot closer to him. It was as if we'd revealed to each other for the first time the way we wanted ourselves to be seen.

I let myself feel again that small, posed moment of tenderness. Maybe that's what closeness really was. We could all keep waiting to come across something more visceral, more real, but reality was always strung up in the performative wires of living itself. Better to take it all at face value, without digging around in constant agitation to find something more beneath it. Better not to idealize love, or desire, or affection. Perhaps the cookbook author and I really were as intimate as her collusive attitude had implied when she'd stood by me. Perhaps she had the right idea, eating whatever she thought best in private, but maintaining a veggie, leggy exterior. At least it got people to eat more vegetables, and gave them hope. And perhaps Lana too really was sincere, her nakedly self-promoting efforts simply an honest reflection of this sincerity.

Lana had stopped talking. We stood watching the dancing crowd, and above them, the projector flashed through the photos from the competition events. The photo of me with the cookbook author came up, and seeing it, I felt exposed yet also gratified in a small way. "Hey, that's you," Lana said, then looked at me and smiled.

It was time for the winner to be revealed. The dance music faded out, the finalists were lined up center stage, and the emcee who'd introduced the videos earlier started officiating. He was a good-looking guy, a host on some small cable show, but he was clearly drunk now, his eyelids at half-mast. "We've really run

these women through the gauntlet," he said, "though I personally would have liked a mud-wrestling contest." A few people
tittered. After another minute or so of this the older emcee
from the morning took over the mic, somewhat forcibly, and
walked us through the judging process. The crowd that until a
few minutes ago had been dancing sweatily against each other
now stood in lonely, self-conscious postures, waiting unhappily.

Unhappy, bored: This was how people really felt about environmentalism and its killjoy mentality, I thought, feeling smug.
At the same time my appreciation for Lana grew. So she was
showoff-y, but so what? There was a vague emptiness at the center of Lana's message that still bothered me, but she was smart
in her own way, strategic, and deserved the mic more than the
boob slurring about mud-wrestling, or the tight-lipped guy
droning on about carbon emissions now, unaware of the mood
of the crowd.

In the end I was glad Lana won the competition. It wasn't so
much that she'd managed to win as that she'd decided to win
from the start, to make that firm grab, and the tenacity and
certainty of that was refreshing, so unlike the wishy-washy, I'll
try and hope for the best-ness of the rest of us. Watching Lana
hold that little trophy above her head, both arms raised and
chest thrust out like in a gymnast finish, I did feel a little proud
of her. I liked her even more when, after her husband came up
and gave her a congratulations hug, she stepped away from him

with a hint of irritation and held the trophy aloft again to dying applause. This was a big moment for her, winning this tiny environmental competition, and seeing that made me feel protective of her happiness.

After that the crowd dispersed. There was a long queue out front for the valet, and waiting in it holding my ticket, I saw the raw cookbook author on the good-looking emcee's arm, giggling as she got into his car, a silver convertible. She turned and saw me watching her. "Oh hey!" she said brightly. She pointed vaguely in the direction of the emcee, who was walking around to the driver's side. "He's giving me a ride home," she said. "Uh-huh," I said, and she blushed a little, and shrugged. Then they were off into the night, the red taillights blinking on and off cheerily.

The next morning I had several emails from Lana. Each one was long and a little strange. One asked that I not mention the word "model" in my article, never mind that the tagline for the competition had been "Be a model for the environment." She said that as the winner, she was trying to do something different, that she was really positioning herself as an intelligent voice for the cause. The word "model," she felt, would undermine her efforts, so she'd appreciate my help with this. I sent back a rather caustic email, to the effect that she could do her job, and I would do mine. At this she wrote back that she understood, she certainly hadn't meant to step on my toes. "You determine how the world sees this," she wrote. "I trust you'll do the right thing."

The world. I scoffed, at her, and also at myself. Lana didn't seem to realize how little my article mattered, even in the small scheme of things. Then on reflection, I thought maybe she was right to be concerned, to try to do what she could to shape how she'd be portrayed. Sure, only a few thousand people would bother to read my write-up, but anyone, at any time, would be able to google it. Perhaps she was wise, more cognizant than I of the web's panopticon. I googled her name with the word "model," and saw that the phrase immediately brought up all the softcore porn photos on the first page, and at that I felt a little sorry for her, her feeble, belated attempt to separate her past and present personae. I emailed back saying I thought she'd be happy with the piece, and apologized that it would be an online-only article. I said that the magazine was trying to expand its web presence and hinted that its web traffic was not high, and I imagined Lana reading this and feeling both disappointed and relieved.

I realized this was how I felt about my own work. It wasn't much, but I had my small little place in the world, and there was a certain freedom in being out of the limelight. I recalled again the night Alek and I found his car using the camera kiosk. Driving to my place afterwards, I told him I had mixed feelings about the cameras. I was thinking back to high school, when cars were about the most private spaces we had. Where did teenagers have sex these days, I wondered. I wondered if they had less sex, or if the sex was even more furtive and closeted, frightening in the YouTube era. This made me a little sad, though almost immediately I began to deliberate over whether or not a little inhibition may be a good thing, may have been a good thing for me.

"Why mixed feelings?" Alek asked.

I deliberated for a moment. "It prevents a certain freedom of imagination," I said. I'd meant it as an innuendo though I wasn't sure he'd get it. A lot of jokes in English still sailed right past him.

He smiled though. "Tell me what you're imagining," he said, and squeezed my thigh. I laughed, and he slid his hand up, bunching my skirt. For a second I thought about stopping him, then decided not to. Whoever was watching the cameras would never see us in real life anyway. And in any case, the cameras weren't watching us. They were watching the cars.

Glow

The night after the night we broke up, Alek showed up at my doorstep unannounced. He pounded on the door, yelling my name. For some reason my first reaction was to look at the clock. It was eight, time for his Saturday AA meeting. My next reaction was to get up and quickly open the door to stop the banging. Alek and I stared at each other in the sudden quiet. He looked strange and familiar across the doorjamb. It was the first time I'd seen him drunk.

"I want to go to the beach," he said slurrily, his Russian accent thicker. "Like first time. For closure."

It was September and a chilly breeze was coming in from the ocean. Above us I could hear the helicopter that had been circling the neighborhood since noon. During the day it had sounded lazy and droning, but now it imbued the dark with a foreboding turbulence. Behind Alek I could see my neighbor's cat across the shared mini patio, staring at us from behind the mesh of the screen door. When she saw me, she pawed at the mesh like she was saying hello.

Alek made a motion like he was going to come in and I stepped to the center of the doorframe, stopping him. We had broken up, and I didn't want the boundaries to get fuzzy again.

"Okay," he said. "Come out. Let's go to the beach." He used that gruff, take it or leave it tone he'd used each time he'd told me he didn't want a serious relationship, not yet. But this time his unfocused eyes were liquid and pleading. His jaw was slack.

"You've been drinking," I said disapprovingly. Still, the muted fascination in my voice was obvious. I couldn't help it. It crept in whenever I learned something new about him, even if it was something I didn't want to hear.

Alek held up his hands as if I was pointing a gun at him. "I've stopped already," he said. His fingers were splayed, like jazz hands. "Stopped," he repeated rather loudly, and at that my neighbor came to his screen door and picked up his cat.

My neighbor was a kindly older man who shared the tomatoes from his container garden with me in the summers. He raised his hand in a wave, like his cat had done.

"You kids going to beach?" my neighbor asked. He called us kids though Alek and I were both in our mid-thirties. "It's Glow tonight, you know."

Alek and I had met at Barnes & Noble, the one on Third Street Promenade. He'd helped me lift down a Vivian Maier tome I couldn't reach. He said he was there looking for a book about self-publishing on Amazon. "But I was distracted by you," he said, smiling, though I'd been the one to talk to him first. He looked very European to me, in his teal jeans and V-neck shirt. His posture was jaunty but intense, his presence visceral, physical. "You're in the wrong section," I said. "You're lost."

He kept smiling. "Yes," he said. "You win."

He suggested taking a walk, first to the pier, then down the beach. The sand was empty but still warm from the summer heat. We'd found an abandoned volleyball and kicked it around, then kissed leaning against lifeguard tower twenty-five.

Since then, a year had passed. Now I said I'd only go to the beach if I drove, and Alek handed me his keys like this was our usual habit, like we'd been sharing a car for some time. The intimacy of this gesture unnerved me and I complied, walking past my car to get into his, opening the passenger door for him from the inside because his automatic locks didn't work, hadn't worked since before we'd met.

Glow was a big, interactive art exhibit on the beach that the city put on one night a year, an event I'd never bothered to go to in the past. Because of the traffic we parked pretty far south and walked up the beach. Giddy young people biked by us in energetic clusters, laughing and yelling over their shoulders, imbuing the air around them with an alert electricity. There were many walkers too; we passed some and were passed by some, all of us moving expectantly toward the Ferris wheel on the pier, its LED lights scrolling through sharp, geometric swirls. Alek took my hand and I didn't resist him. His energy felt angry and unpredictable and incoherently masochistic, and I thought my literal hold on him would give me some control over his actions.

My hand did seem to have a pacifying effect. Alek moved closer to me as the crowds thickened, walking politely, careful not to step on anyone's heels. I'd never seen the beach this packed before; we missed the first exhibit entirely because it was completely hidden behind a long wall of waiting people. Gentle hordes clustered like bees around the big lit globes that marked each exhibit, and milled about reading the sign before splintering off into small groups and wading industriously through the loose sand, toward the actual artworks.

Alek and I tromped to the first exhibit we spotted. It looked like a gigantic net hanging down from the sky in messy parabolas, lit up in changing, luminous colors. Below it, the sand had been sculpted into hills and valleys. Little boys busied themselves running up and down these moldings. Clusters of teenagers sat in the low points, possessively hoarding the shadowy areas, trying to mask their youthful enthusiasm with cultivated postures of apathy. The more adult stood shoulder to shoulder on the high ridges, watching the colors morph on the nets and occasionally looking around at each other. I looked around too; there was the sense that something else was supposed to happen, though nothing did.

Alek asked if I was cold, then put his arms around me. He smelled like vodka but he felt the way he always did, which comforted me. He said we should go by the water so we did, and he held me there as we watched the little waves come in. He said he was glad to be out, then added, "with you."

Twenty-four hours before we'd been lying naked in my bed, not touching. We'd just had sex, then the half-dozenth argument about whether or not we were "committed." He'd said he wasn't seeing anyone else and wasn't going to. I'd said I couldn't take him referring to me as his "friend" anymore, that this behavior was juvenile. We'd argued for a while and then we'd fallen silent. After some time he'd said, "Do you want me to go?" In the past I'd sometimes hedged this question, sometimes said okay, then when he called my bluff, reduced myself to begging him to stay. But I was angry this night, a year to the day since we'd met. I got up and got dressed. Then I held the door open until he got dressed too. When he finally stepped outside I said, "Wait," and he stopped expectantly. I ran to the bathroom and got his toothbrush. I handed it to him and turned on the porch light. "Watch your step," I said, pointing my chin at the stairs. I saw his face shift, harden. Then I closed the door.

Now here we were, on the sand again. I was wearing old jeans and a shapeless hoodie, what I'd had on when Alek had started banging on the door. I was embarrassed by my shabby outfit but Alek didn't seem to notice. I'd taken off my shoes and my feet were cold in the sand. I shivered a little. Alek zipped up my hoodie, then hugged me tightly. His lips pressed against my ear, slack and wet. "This is not me," he said, whispering. "You know this is not me. I call my sponsor tomorrow." He paused. "Tonight."

I put my arms around him too. There was a new tenderness to him I wanted to wallow in. He seemed to be sobering up. Before this Alek had been sober four years and counting. Or maybe three years, since there was that slip up that had landed him back in detox that he'd mentioned once, in passing. I wasn't sure. I could never figure out the timeline of his biography because his math was always fuzzy. He mentioned often the rigorous honesty part of the twelve-step program but he also told a lot of lies of omission. I'd fallen for him because he was affectionate and spontaneous and generous. He'd brought flowers and encouraged my writing and cooked for me when I was sick. It was only once I got comfortable that he revealed he wasn't divorced, that in fact he was so newly separated that he hadn't even found a place yet, he was living out of his office. The separation had wrecked his credit, he confessed. Then one day he showed me a video of his five-year-old daughter twirling in a tutu. He showed me this in such a vulnerable way that I felt closer to him and forgave his secrecy. The daughter lived in Palos Verdes with her mother, who'd gotten Alek his US citizenship and who was still legally his wife, though he never referred to her as such. I'd realized soon after that he also never referred to me as his girlfriend.

Once we got back to my place, our feet were gritty and we were both tired but we still moved toward each other with a tender resolve. Our motions as we undressed felt obligatory, but affectionate too, in its doggedness. Still, once we were naked, I kept getting distracted. I remembered Alek's big smile at the bookstore, like he couldn't believe his incredible luck, as he entrusted the weight of the Maier tome into my hands. I held that image close as Alek kissed me now, my mouth, my breasts. He went down on me, then after I came, stayed with his face burrowed between my legs. I swiveled my body around and took him in my mouth. I pictured him young, imagined how he'd looked eleven years ago when he'd just moved to California, working as an off-the-books hotel security guard with the San Francisco fog damp in his hair, his attitude impulsive and cocky despite the muted fears about his future. I got that tense, fraught feeling again, like I needed to act quickly, I needed to figure it out before I lost my chance for good. It was then that Alek reached down and softly touched my head. "I can sense your teeth a little bit," he said. His tone as he said this was very gentle, apologetic, and for some reason that suddenly brought into focus the hilarious absurdity of our night, my life. For a second I had the urge to burst out laughing, though the feeling faded, and I didn't.